Vivian's Couch by Michael Obiora

For Juju - SS2 Merms

FREDDIE, 2011

'Abani is a sellout!' came a voice from the crowd.

'Innit, he's a white man!' shouted another.

Freddie Abani kept his poker face on, doing his utmost to appear unfazed by the backlash from his hometown. *These people believe in me,* was the theme of his internal dialogue. He represented these people; he was their voice. On this muggy summer morning, news reporters and cameras surrounded Freddie. There were journalists with notepads and Dictaphones and an angry mob of Woundham residents. There were police lines in front of damaged shops and residential buildings; there was glass and debris on the ground. Remnants of last night's riots littered the high street.

Devon Constance had been gunned down by police hours before the Woundham postcode began to attack, demanding answers. It was 'The Battle of Woundham, 1997' all over again. Back then, tensions in this part of North London were high; the largely black local community didn't trust the Metropolitan Police, and the largely white Metropolitan Police didn't trust the local community. Something had to give; in that case it was the lives of two black women – one from a stroke following an arrest and the other from a police bullet – and the fatal battering of a policeman on the rainy night that followed.

Freddie blinked continuously, attempting to chase the memory from his mind. He looked out towards the press and spoke. 'Let me make one thing clear, this is not a black and white thing—'

'Of course it's not!' an unidentified female voice interrupted from the baying mob. 'White people don't like you either!'

Freddie swallowed hard and tried to ignore the sniggers. 'Woundham has made great strides over the last fifteen years. And the mindless nihilism of a small group has threatened to undo all the hard work that has gone into building bridges between the community and the police.' Freddie adjusted the spectacles on the bridge of his nose. 'I have lived here almost all my life—'

'Yeah, yeah, coconut.'

Ignore them. 'And it hurts to see my town damaged like this.' Freddie continued. 'Devon Constance's family understandably wants answers, and so does the community. This began with a peaceful protest—'

'It began with a murder!'

Freddie had to raise his voice to overcome the murmurs of agreement that came from the latest outburst. 'Yes, there are many questions that the police are going to have to answer. But this chaos threatens to overshadow the justified peaceful protest of Devon's friends and family. I now have a meeting with the head of the Independent Police Complaints Commission—'

'This ain't never gonna stop till we get justice!'

Freddie raised his arms slightly, revealing sweat patches in his armpits. He knew he couldn't stop speaking so he opened his mouth to carry on.

Helen Walters, the head of the local area council, stepped forward. Watching her take up pole position, Freddie licked his dry lips, humiliated by the apparent ease with which the white woman spoke. Her voice faded into the background and

Freddie took what felt like his first breath for an eternity. The smell of burnt rubber advanced up his nostrils and he thought about those left homeless after the kamikaze that had been last night. He placed a hand on his short Afro and looked at the charred independent jewellers across the road. It had been there for over twenty years and now it barely stood, with shattered windows and its contents emptied. Its neighbour, Woundham Electronics, was smashed to pieces. The family business had famously been established in the 1940s, surviving the Second World War, but it hadn't been immune to last night's looters. Freddie tried to imagine how its owner, Mr Alan, was feeling this very moment.

He shut his eyes tightly, momentarily trying to block out the damage, but cries of 'Justice for Devon!' and the echoes of 'Bounty!' and 'Boot licker!' resounded in his head.

The Right Honourable thirty-eight-year-old Freddie Abani, MP for Woundham, the man who was once mooted as potentially the first black Mayor of London, had one more thing to talk to Vivian about.

VIVIAN

They say that the most disciplined people are often a step away from addiction. The phrase 'they' I find to be a curious one. Who is this 'they'? Whoever they are, 'they' may be right in my case.

I'm a recovering alcoholic. Thirty-seven months sober. It wasn't just the abusive marriage I was in that led me to drink. I would have been an addict regardless. The beatings I suffered at the hands of my husband merely triggered it, and then became somewhat of an excuse. Addiction is a personality trait of mine, and acknowledging it was the first step towards my recovery. Removing the trigger was the second. The third step was finding something non-destructive to channel my addiction into. I am now driven by a desire to help people, and to understand the motives behind one's actions. This has helped me learn to forgive my ex- husband. I actually visit him in prison, and talking to him has been very helpful for the both of us. Ironically, we've communicated better since he's been inside. Women are much better at expressing how they feel than their male counterparts. By no means have any of my husband's letters been a diary charting an understanding of his behaviour. But since we've started writing to each other I've found reading his words somewhat therapeutic. It seems to me that he is actually appreciative of the opportunity to try and comprehend the depression that led to the breakdown of our marriage. And although it would probably be unrealistic for me to expect him to communicate as freely with me in person, I myself am grateful that somehow I have found the strength to try and use what has been a very sad

and difficult episode as an opportunity to try to understand people even more …

There was a light tap on the door, and Vivian put her diary away in her desk
drawer.

RUPAL, MONDAY 11 A.M.

'… and I was sick of it.' Rupal lay on the couch, with her hands placed over her
shut eyelids. '"Terrorist … you're not even from here, bitch", all sorts. It's one thing
receiving this kind of abuse from some members of the public – unfortunately you
get used to it after a while – but how could I be treated like this by my colleagues?'

Vivian nodded.

'But I can't help thinking that I let them win,' Rupal continued. 'You know what I
mean? That I let their ignorance get the better of me.' She sat up on the couch
and opened her eyes. 'What am I going to do with my life now?'

Vivian leaned towards the coffee table that separated her from Rupal, and
topped up her patient's glass with water.

Before continuing, Rupal took a sip. 'My parents keep bleating on about how I
should just admit that they were right, and that everything will be better if I just
marry a nice Indian boy from "back home". I mean, what is this? Why couldn't they
applaud me for trying to make a difference?'

'What do you mean by difference?' Vivian asked.

The question seemed to stop Rupal in her tracks. 'You know?' Rupal said with an expression of confusion on her face. 'In my job, as a police woman?'

'Right,' Vivian said, writing in her file.

Rupal looked at her, annoyed at the interruption. 'It's always my bloody older brother who gets the praise. All he does is go to the temple and talk to me about how I need to clean up my life.' Rupal took a brief pause, as if she was waiting for Vivian to comment. When she was satisfied Vivian wasn't ready to speak, she continued. 'I'm twenty-bloody-seven years old, and it would be a problem to bring my boyfriend home because he is white. I mean, what the fuck is that?!'

'Why do you remain at home?' Vivian asked.

Rupal flicked a thick lock of her jet-black hair behind her ear. 'What do you mean?'

'Well' – Vivian rested her file on her dark-brown thighs – 'You clearly have no problem removing yourself from difficult situations, as demonstrated by your leaving your job.'

Rupal stared at Vivian. 'Technically, I live with George.'

'Your boyfriend?' Vivian asked.

Rupal nodded.

'I see,' said Vivian, regarding her. 'Why is the approval of your parents so important to you?'

Rupal's gaze now went past Vivian, somewhere into the distance, and after what seemed like a long silence, she said, 'At the end of the day, they're my family. I love them.'

KIERAN AND CALLUM, 1998

Callum gasped in mock horror. 'You're going to be in trouble. Mum just washed that!' He was talking to Kieran, his little brother, who had just completed a front-facing belly slide on the damp autumn grass. The two boys had been enjoying their after-school kickabout at the park. This was one of the things Kieran looked forward to most. As soon as the school bell rang, he would rush to the front gates, football in hand, and wait for his older brother. Once Callum joined him – after-school detention permitting – the ritual would continue as they ran to Green Hill Park.

'Come on, Cal,' Kieran said, rubbing his mud-stained shirt, spreading the dirt even more. 'I had to celebrate getting to one hundred and fifty kick ups!'

'Alright, alright, stop showing off,' Callum replied, adjusting his school tie, which was now wrapped around his forehead.

'I'm going to go for two hundred this time!' Kieran said as he skilfully flicked the ball up with his feet.

'No, this is getting boring. Anyway, Mum and Dad said I'm in charge, and I say we have to go home now.'

'Please, ten more minutes!' Kieran appealed, his eyes remaining fixed on the ball as he dribbled around an invisible defender.

'No!' And with that, Callum snatched the ball with both hands and ran off, scooping up his backpack along the way.

'Hey!' Kieran shouted, giving chase.

'You can't catch me!' Callum giggled, 'I'm too big and too strong! Last one home is a stinking weakling!'

Despite the obvious difference of their skin colour, the stepbrothers were also quite different personalities. The white one, fourteen-year-old Callum, was naughty. This trait of his had developed over the last six years or so. It had been six years ago that his parents, Nigel and Anna Ledley, had adopted mixed-race Kieran. Suddenly no longer an only child, Callum began to play up. This continued into the early years of secondary school. While the shy, cute Kieran was the talk of the family, always in the centre of all the photographs – 'Oh wow, look at his lovely hair', 'What soft skin he has' – Callum was busy swearing at teachers and pushing over the smaller kids in his class.

Callum was tall for his age, with mousey brown hair, and he gradually became louder and more aggressive as he turned into a teenager.

Eleven-year-old Kieran was one of the smallest in his class.

Skinny, and shy, Callum would often come to his rescue when his little brother was tripped up or called names by his peers. 'Yellow monkey!', 'Half-baked Jaffa Cake!' some of the boys and girls of the inner-city comprehensive would shout.

No problem for Callum; at lunchtime another bully would be dealt with by him.
'He's not even really your brother,' fifteen-year-old Rob Smith wheezed, holding
his ribs after a beat down from Callum – yes, Callum sometimes beat up kids in
the older years on Kieran's behalf. 'Monkey lover,' Rob Smith called as he limped
away.

Callum enjoyed coming to his brother's aid. Despite his now mounting
suspensions, it made him feel important. This was more than could be said for the
dynamics in the Ledley household. It was always Kieran being hugged first. It was
always Kieran who occupied the coveted spot beside his father on the couch, in
front of the TV. And to top it off, Kieran was now spending more and more time
with Nigel on the way to football training.

'I'm a little worried about Callum,' Anna would say as she lay next to her
husband in bed.

'He's just going through a phase,' Callum would overhear his father reply.

'Do you think we're giving him enough attention?'

'He'll be fine. Anyway, it's getting late. Early start for Kieran's trial tomorrow. It's
going to be an important day.'

And so it would go; the conversation would always end with Kieran. Precious
little future footy star.

He's not even that good, Callum would say to himself, staring at the ceiling.
He's too small – sports stars can't be weak. Callum would then look over to his
little brown brother, who was sleeping in the other bed, wishing he could be him.
Things were better before the black one came along.

GEMMA AND PETE, WEDNESDAY 6 P.M.

'Deep down, I don't really think he cares.' Gemma's arms were crossed tightly. 'He doesn't give a fuck about me. I could sleep with every man on our street and he still wouldn't give a shit.'

Pete let out a short sigh and clasped his hands above his knees. For the past seven minutes he had been sat in this position, his eyes fixed on Vivian's burgundy carpet.

'Unbelievable.' Gemma gave Vivian an incredulous smile before looking back to her husband on the couch beside her. 'Well, say something, you prick.'

'If I didn't give a shit, I wouldn't be here, would I?' These were Pete's first words in this evening's session since he'd greeted Vivian at the door.

Gemma clicked her fingers in front of his face. 'Communicate with me. How am I supposed to know if you don't talk to me?' She looked across to Vivian for support before turning back towards him and patronisingly saying,

'Communication.'

Pete rubbed his wide face and mumbled something.

'What was that?' Gemma asked, in the passive-aggressive tone she would

occasionally adopt in front of the therapist.

'Nothing,' Pete replied. He hadn't looked at her once since they'd sat down. In

fact, it was becoming more difficult for Pete to remember the last time he had

actually looked at his wife. Even if Pete could remember, he knew it had been

years since he had actually seen her.

The woman sat beside him wasn't the woman he'd married. She was a beast.

A monster created by the fact that she had sacrificed her life for him. Pete

Newman, the award-winning British film-maker. The man whose career was ready

to go stratospheric after his crowning moment: winning Best International Film at

the American Film Critics Guild Awards. His acceptance speech had gone down

as one of the highlights of that night three years ago.

He had thanked his 'beautiful wife', his 'rock', 'my reason for living'. Gemma had

looked on from the auditorium, applauding, letting a tear travel down her cheek.

She was happy for her husband. His journey to this moment had almost cost them

their marriage. They had survived, but what was next? Gemma wondered. She

knew that Pete wouldn't rest on his laurels now. She knew that he would embark

on a mission to 'seize the moment'. That was one of his mottos, and he

obsessively put it into practice now that he was an award-winning film-maker. The trips to Los Angeles, and other international destinations, for 'meetings' became more frequent. Gemma accompanying her husband on these trips became less so. She was jealous. She hadn't bargained on sharing her husband with the world. She hadn't put in all these years of financial struggle, upheaval, moving into a new place every six months, telling her crying husband that he was talented – 'They will all see soon' – just to be abandoned. She hadn't spent all this time picking him up off the floor, for him to leave her by the wayside.

There was only one way to get their marriage back on track: have a baby.

'Soon,' Pete would promise. 'Once we finalise this deal.' The deal in question was a big studio movie that was sure to be the big break in Hollywood he had been waiting for. His first foray into the mainstream movie world. His transition from British film-maker to a Hollywood big shot. After ten months of trips back and forth, the deal never materialised. And neither had the baby Gemma yearned for.

They were now right back where they started. A couple living in London, drowning in debt. Every promise that had been made to the award-winning Pete Newman had been broken. His phone no longer needed to be charged three times a day for all the ringing. His agent was suddenly too busy to talk; the interest from the Americans had 'cooled'. There was nothing left of the moment to seize.

Here they were, sat having marriage counselling, weathered. Gemma, once energetic, now worn down with all the mothering she had to do with Pete. Soaked in resentment towards the man who had promised to look after her 'as soon as things were sorted.' The man whom she gave up work for – how could she keep a job when she was constantly living out of a suitcase? She had lost count of the amount of beds they had slept in over the last eighteen months, how many hotels they had stayed at, hotels they couldn't afford. Why couldn't Pete see the damage his so-called career had caused to their marriage?

Why did his mind always seem to be elsewhere when she spoke to him? Why was he more interested in an upcoming meeting than his wife? When – Gemma would ask herself at night, as her husband slept with his back facing her – would he stop putting their life on hold for a job that was 'around the corner'?

If he wasn't going to let them have a baby, if he wasn't going to acknowledge how much she had put into their marriage, Gemma's next act was sure to get his attention; and this is when her series of affairs with other men started.

'Pete?'

On hearing his name called by Vivian, he looked up. 'Is there anything more you think you can do to show your wife that you care about her actions?'

'He's only here so he can say that he's trying,' Gemma chimed in.

'Gemma,' Vivian said calmly, 'we've spoken about you letting your husband talk.'

'If we keep waiting for that,' Gemma snorted, 'the whole bloody session would be over.'

Vivian observed the couple in front of her. Pete, early forties, a few pounds overweight. His alcohol bloated face always had a pink and red tone to it. He had a full head of brown hair and a large jaw that hung slightly open. Almost as if he was a little out of breath.

Gemma had the look of a woman who was probably the prettiest in the class when she was at school. She had big brown eyes, and even though they had bags below them, one could see that they once had a spark. Her dark hair was cut into a neat bob, a symbol of the effort that she would fight to make.

Vivian had noticed that she had become a little paler in recent weeks, that her eyeballs were becoming redder with each session, and that she had dropped a little weight from her already slim frame.

'I just think that we need to be more settled before we have a baby,' Pete said.

Vivian observed him softly say these words towards the ground. She vaguely remembered watching him on television picking up his award and delivering his speech with such confidence. The man in front of her was a shadow of that image.

'When will that be?!' Gemma shouted. 'When will we be settled? I'm thirty-nine. I'm not getting any younger. You were supposed to look after me! You haven't touched me in years. How dare you?! You fat prick! How dare you?!'

Her eyes filled with tears as she trembled. She stormed over to the door, grabbing a tissue from the side table on the way.

'Gemma, we made a real breakthrough last week when you agreed—'

'No!' Gemma interrupted Vivian, dabbing at her tears with the tissue. She turned to Pete and pointed at him. 'That's why I fucked Steve and Tim! That's why.'

She left the room, slamming the door behind her.

KIERAN, 2011

Kieran lay on the bed, only slightly panting, in contrast to Nathan who was significantly out of breath. Nathan sat on the edge of the bed smoking a joint. He looked at Kieran. 'You wanna hit?' he asked, waving the roll-up.

'Yeah,' Kieran mumbled.

Nathan handed the joint over to his client and watched him take a long drag. 'That's it, son, smile.'

Nathan was Kieran's agent. He'd looked after Kieran since he'd turned professional at sixteen years old.

Nathan guarded his star client jealously, making sure that whatever Kieran wanted, Kieran got. High-class hookers? Check. The arrangement of an abortion after a one-night stand? Check. A journalist that had to be paid off? Check. And if Kieran needed a 'lift' in drug form, as long as it was outside of the drug-testing period, Nathan would take care of it. With the random drugs test rules in the Premier League, Kieran's highs were becoming more risky, so Nathan would make sure that clean urine was at the ready for his client.

There was no way that he would let any harm come to the product he'd taken from child prodigy and turned into a millionaire superstar football player. Agent supreme Nathan Rougel had brokered the seventy million pound transfer of Kieran Ledley from Albans Town to Authenton FC. He had 'cut' his fee down to one per cent of the transfer. The rest was made up of the ten per cent he received from Kieran's signing-on fee, which was a reported six million pounds. Kieran was always very generous to Nathan. He unfailingly responded positively to Nathan's requests that he 'look after' his agent. After all, how could Kieran ever argue? Who was it that negotiated his one hundred and ninety-five thousand pound a week wage? Who was it that made sure every endorsement he took on was rewarded with at least six figures?

Kieran's biological father went AWOL after his birth, and although Mr Ledley senior had made several attempts to contact his now incredibly rich and famous son, as far as Nathan was concerned, he was Kieran's only father (although in front of Nigel he was careful to not go any further than saying, 'You, Anna, and I want the best for Kieran in equal measure.'). So it was only right that Kieran made his agent a millionaire too.

'Bloody hell, is she dead in there?' said Nathan, taking the joint from Kieran before making his way across the five star hotel suite to the bathroom door.

'Love?' He knocked on the door and turned to Kieran. 'What's her name again?'

'What?' Kieran said, sitting up on the bed and rubbing his temples.

'In there.' Nathan gestured over his shoulder to the bathroom. He half-heartedly attempted a whisper, 'What's the bird's name?'

Kieran shrugged and headed over to the window.

Nathan turned back to the door. 'Babe, you still alive in there?'

'Yeah, just a sec,' said a female voice from the other side of the door.

'Good.' Nathan saw Kieran staring out of the window. 'Son?' he called from across the room. When Kieran turned to face him, Nathan said, 'Who says roasts are only for Sundays, eh?'

Kieran feigned a smile and Nathan beamed back a devilish grin. 'That's the spirit! Well played, son!'

The sound of a toilet flushing came from the bathroom and a naked, twenty-something-year-old pretty girl walked past Nathan into the room. She didn't flinch as he slapped her behind, simply running her hands through her dishevelled, bottle-blonde hair.

Kieran handed the girl her underwear and called to Nathan, 'Sort her a cab, will you?'

Nathan took one last hit of the dwindling roll-up. 'Done.' He brought out his phone and went into the bathroom.

Kieran reached under the bed and retrieved his boxers.

'Tish,' the girl said, watching Kieran slide them on.

Kieran gave her a quizzical look.

'My name's Tish.'

Kieran nodded, and the girl slipped back into her tiny black dress.

Nathan returned to the room rubbing his middle-age spread. 'Love, the driver's in the lobby.'

'Tish.'

'Huh?' Nathan said as he lazily threw the rest of his clothes on.

'My name's Tish.'

'Great. I'll walk you down.' He rolled his eyes at Kieran and guided Tish to the door, before following her out.

Kieran picked the remnants of the joint off the carpet, and threw it out the window. He closed his eyes and took a deep breath. He looked down into the night and stared at the tiny moving lights below, slowly drifting like glittering fish in a black ocean. This was home away from home. The twelfth floor, master suite of the City Panoramic Hotel. The place where he would roast any day of the week, and often contemplate diving out of the window, down into the black sea.

Kieran's thoughts of suicide were interrupted by the buzz of his mobile phone. He turned back into the room and searched for the phone on the messy bed. He found it and looked at the screen. The illuminated display read '*WIFEY*'.

He looked on, expressionless, as the moniker of his smiling fiancée stared back at him.

FREDDIE, THURSDAY 1 P.M.

'I can't believe this has happened in my constituency … I feel let down, embarrassed … and I actually feel like I've let the people down, too.' Freddie undid the top button of his grey shirt. He removed his glasses and placed them on the coffee table between himself and Vivian.

'How can you feel responsible in any way for the reaction to Devon's death?' Vivian asked, sat across from him.

'It's my home town!' Freddie shouted, betraying his public persona of calm.

Vivian didn't find it difficult to distinguish between her patients who enjoyed therapy and those who loathed it. She knew that Freddie belonged in the former category. It was clear that he appreciated being able to let his guard down. They had often discussed the stress of keeping up appearances. Freddie lamented the fact that outside of his home, when he wasn't with his wife and two sons, he couldn't be himself. And for an hour every Thursday he would do all he could to exorcise this feeling.

'I know Devon's partner, Hailey, and their three-year-old son ...' Freddie's eyes were welling up. He paused and reached into his blazer beside him. He pulled out a handkerchief and wiped his face. 'Another black boy without a father.'

Vivian pursed her lips and looked at Freddie sympathetically. She considered the MP. 'Are you ready to—'

Freddie looked up sharply. 'No, I'm not ready to talk about my dad.'

Vivian successfully concealed her frustration. 'We made a breakthrough last week, Freddie.'

'It's not about him.' Freddie replied with a shake of his head.

Vivian leaned back on her sofa. 'What is it about?'

Freddie picked his glasses up from the table and put them on. 'It's about the fact that an unarmed black man was shot dead by the police, and I'm supposed to condemn the riots that ensued.'

'So you agree with the riots?' Vivian asked.

'No, I don't agree with the bloody riots! What's burning down local businesses and ruining innocent people's livelihoods going to do? It's not about that!'

'So what is it about?' Vivian probed.

'I'll tell you what it's about!' Freddie yelled, jumping to his feet. 'It's about the fact that I care about Woundham but the resident's don't think that I do because I'm apparently some expenses fiddling, out of touch, wealthy politician. It's about the fact that I went out and got an education so that I could be independent and fight for justice. It's about the fact that I'm being called a "white man" when I'm trying to represent these people. It's about the fact that I'm collectively thought of as a "sellout" for having a white wife. It's about the fact that almost none of my constituents look like me. That they make me cringe when they refer to people as "coloured". That I'm in the middle of what the media are trying to paint as an act of black angst. It's about the fucking fact that whether he was a drug dealer or not, an unarmed twenty-seven-year-old black man has been slain by the police and he's left behind a fiancée and a little black boy who is going to grow up without a father-figure, just like I did!'

Vivian looked at Freddie. He was out of breath, and his trademark sweat patches leaked through his shirt. She wrote something down before saying, 'Thank you, Freddie. That's the end of our session today.'

Freddie looked around Vivian's office, as if he had been awoken from a trance.

'Really?' he asked disappointedly, looking at his watch.

Vivian nodded.

Freddie cleared his throat and picked up his blazer. As he closed the door behind him, Vivian smiled softly.

RUPAL, MONDAY 11 A.M.

'It got to the point where I'd dread my colleagues asking me for a drink at the end of our shifts because I wanted to go to George's and smoke a joint.'

Vivian wrote in her file before looking back up at Rupal. 'So, smoking marijuana is something that started off recreationally between you and your partner George?'

Rupal tossed her thick black hair over her right shoulder and smiled ruefully. 'Yeah. We used to make jokes about the irony of me "fighting crime" and then spending the nights smoking weed.'

Vivian flicked back through her file before resting on a page. 'You say that you were actually encouraged to occasionally smoke by your colleagues in the police force. To alleviate stress.'

Rupal nodded. There was a brief moment of silence before she said, '"Occasionally" being the operative word.'

Vivian topped up Rupal's glass of water.

Rupal shook her head slowly. 'It's the guilt.'

'How do you mean?' Vivian asked.

'I remember when my parents used to call me at university, to see how I was. My mum used to say things like "You better not be smoking drugs. I hope you're not being influenced by those English wasters."' Rupal chuckled slightly, seemingly amused by her impression of her mother's accent.

Vivian smiled and looked at Rupal quizzically.

'Don't you get it?' Rupal asked.

Vivian squinted and remained silent.

Rupal let out an irritated sigh. 'It always comes back to colour with them. Drugs, alcohol. According to my mum and dad, these were what white people did. God forbid an Asian person – let alone their daughter – would engage in such activities.' Rupal sat back into the sofa and took a deep breath.

'And that's where the guilt comes in?' Vivian asked, knowingly.

Rupal nodded. 'Smoking dope with my white boyfriend.'

Vivian placed the file on the desk behind her. 'We all have our vices, Rupal. I suppose the worst thing is when we don't acknowledge them. But in your case you have.'

Rupal's face lit up. 'Exactly. How dare they, or anyone else, fucking judge me? Nobody has any idea the kind of pressure I've been put under since I was a child. Living in my brother's shadow. Having my future mapped out for me by my parents.' Rupal once again adopted an Indian accent. '"You must go to medical school. We'll show those Advanis that they're not the only ones with smart children!" I was fucking sick of it!'

Vivian calmly crossed her legs. She took in the sight of Rupal panting and wondered whether she would have noticed the dark circles around her pretty patient's eyes if marijuana hadn't been mentioned. 'Do you think that's why you dropped out of university to join the police force?'

Rupal frowned and took a sip of her water.

'Justice?' Vivian continued. 'Perhaps you felt trapped and because of this felt the need to seek justice.'

Rupal slowly ran a hand through her hair, and then down over her cheek. 'I don't know,' she said. 'All I know is that I feel guilty for not going to medical school, I feel guilty for quitting the force, and I'm not sure if I'm only with George to piss my parents off.'

They sat in silence until Rupal looked at her watch and stood up. 'I'm tired, Vivian. I'm always tired. And the only thing that helps me sleep is a big bag of weed.'

CALLUM, 2003

Callum looked on with a mix of pride and envy as history was being made. His younger brother jogged on the spot, wearing a nervous expression.

Callum stood up and pointed at the flickering television screen. 'That's my little bro!'

'Sit down, man!' Tiny grumbled, his large frame contradicting his name.

'Yeah, get your big head out the way!' Another voice came from behind.

'Shut up! That's my fucking little brother!'

'And my girlfriend's a supermodel! Now sit your wasted self down.'

Callum turned back towards the television and sat down, giving Tiny and all those behind him the finger.

'... and here he comes, Kieran Ledley, making his first team debut for Albans Town. At sixteen years and sixty-two days, he's the youngest ever player in the Premier League.'

Callum looked on as his stepbrother ran onto the pitch. He thought about how different their lives had become. Here he was, seventeen months into his two-and-a-half-year sentence for armed robbery, watching his brother embark on his career as a professional football player. Callum had been on his best behaviour lately, hence this treat. All the inmates watching today's game were being rewarded for completing various tasks, and the mood was good. Apart from the odd insult here and there from supporters of one team to another, it seemed everyone was happy. But at that moment, Callum couldn't have felt sadder.

KIERAN, 2011

'Mr Ledley.' 'Kieran.' 'This way Mr Ledley.' 'Over here.'

Kieran squinted, blinded by the lights. A grinning Nathan was sat on his right, with his new club's manager and coach, Alan Turble, on his left. It was only seconds ago that Authenton FC's Chairman, Donald Kleens, had said that they were now taking questions, but the room had erupted into a chorus of requests.

'One at a time please, we'll get through as many as possible.'

'Kieran!' Somebody shouted from the back.

Kieran squinted his eyes further as he attempted to find the owner of the voice amongst the sea of sports writers and journalists.

'Kieran! Has it always been a dream of yours to play for Authenton or was it the sizeable wage that tempted you?'

The other members of the press settled down, demonstrating their collective desire for an answer.

'Erm, I ...'

'Many people are saying that you would have gone anywhere for two hundred grand a week—'

'We are not prepared to talk about Kieran's pay packet today,' Nathan said in a calm and professional manner.

'Okay, can you tell us if the reported figures are completely wide of the mark or —'

'Like Mr Rougel said,' Donald, the chairman, chimed in, 'we will not be discussing Kieran's wages in any way, shape, or form.'

Kieran looked at his agent and his new bosses, Alan and Donald, and then he thought about the club's absent new owners, the Karim brothers. He didn't know much about these investors; only that they dealt in oil and had flown him and Nathan out to Dubai earlier in the summer after a season of much speculation; that they were prepared to make him the highest-paid football player on the planet; that they would be happy to smash the transfer record for him; that they would stop at nothing to get 'the world's best player'; and that they would make sure that he and Nathan would be taken care of for the rest of their lives.

Kieran knew that today was the day his life would change forever. It was no longer 'playing for the love of the game'. This was beyond that. He was now a brand, and a lot of people's livelihoods rested on his shoulders.

He sat behind a table on a raised platform, dressed in a dark tailored suit. This choice of clothing was Nathan's. It was all business from this moment on. 'You are now going to transcend football, and you have to look the part,' was what he would say leading up to this press conference. And Kieran didn't argue with his mentor and agent.

'Mr Ledley,' said a female voice.

Kieran looked towards the pretty dark-haired female journalist who was now standing.

'How do you feel you are going to be able to cope with your record-breaking price tag?' She held a Dictaphone towards the raised platform.

'Kieran's—'

'Hang on,' Kieran said, holding a hand up to Nathan, whose grin momentarily lost its shape due to the interruption. 'It's always going to be difficult to justify the huge sums of money in football,' Kieran continued, 'especially in the current climate. But I didn't set my price tag, or wages. I've obviously been doing something right so far, and I'll continue to give my best.'

The female journalist smiled and sat down.

Nathan smiled at Kieran, who was aware that his agent was always worried about letting him speak for himself.

A short, thickset man stood. 'Kieran, Matthew Davis from *Evening Sport*. Those are confident words going forward. Welcome to Authenton. Have you got a message for your former teammates and fans? You denied that you were thinking of leaving all through last season, and even kissed the badge after you scored in what turned out to be your final game for them.'

'Well,' Kieran loosened his tie. He was now beginning to feel the heat from all the lights. 'I just want to thank them for all the support they have given me. They'll always be in my heart.'

'So why did you leave?'

Kieran looked at Nathan before saying, 'It was time for a new challenge.'

'Mr Turble!' Came a voice from the back. 'Are you going to change your system so Kieran can go straight into the team this weekend? Or are you going to make him the world's most expensive substitute?'

A chorus of laughter erupted from the journalists.

Alan Turble remained expressionless. He hadn't been enjoying the circus that had surrounded Kieran's transfer. In fact, he hadn't been happy since the Karim brother's had taken over Authenton and began to put their new regime in place. He had never been consulted about Kieran's transfer. He glanced at Kieran. Two men fighting for control. Alan Turble, the fifty-six-year-old Scotsman who had guided the club into the Champions League for the first time in almost fifteen years. His biggest achievement as a manager was turning out to be the start of his downfall. Constant rumours about who his club were after; countless speculation about which 'big name' manager was being lined up as his replacement; the chairman and agents meeting to discuss transfer targets without his consent. Alan and Kieran were both feeling the pressure of being in the spotlight, but for different reasons.

On the outside Kieran had it all. Clad in his designer suit, looking like a movie star as the sporting world crowned a new king. But he felt like a puppet. He felt like he was a product that had no choice but to deliver.

'Kieran is fully fit and available for selection,' said Alan. 'He will definitely be considered for this weekend's game.'

The journalists laughed again and there was a frosty look between Alan and Donald.

'Kieran, this move is not only big news on the back pages. It's also making noise in the pop world. What part did your fiancée, Clarissa, play in your decision to join the London club?'

'I'm not here to talk about my private life.' Kieran turned to Nathan. He hid his mouth behind his hands and whispered, 'Get me out of here.'

Nathan nodded towards Donald, who then said, 'Okay, we've only got time for a couple more.'

Kieran clenched his jaw and looked out at the journalists. He couldn't hear anything but his name. And he couldn't see anything but flashing lights and a heaving unfriendly mass.

'That was horrendous.' Kieran sat in the passenger seat of Nathan's black Range Rover.

'It wasn't that bad, son,' Nathan replied as he drove.

Looking through the tinted windows at the passing congested city, Kieran shook his head. 'Seriously, that wasn't fun. I just want to get this weekend out of the way.' He stared at the faces that whizzed by, wondering where they were going. He saw a smiling young man holding a small boy's hand at the zebra crossing and wondered whether they were father and son. He saw a couple strolling with their arms around each other, drinking coffees and looking happy and carefree. Kieran thought about the fact that he was probably earning more in a week than the passing crowd would earn in a year. This brought him no joy. He looked at his sombre reflection in the wing mirror and thought about the contrast between his expression and the father and son. Everybody looked so happy.

Nathan had been speaking but Kieran hadn't been listening.

'Do you hear me, son? Son?' Kieran's thoughts were halted by Nathan.

'What?' Kieran said, looking at his expectant agent.

'Stay with me, son. We've got too much riding on this. Do you hear? Keep it together.'

'I am keeping it together. What are you talking about?' Kieran replied defensively.

'You're daydreaming, Kieran. Take it easy. We'll go and have a drink at the hotel – tonic water for you – and an early night for your first training session, okay?'

Kieran reverted to looking out of the tinted window at the typically overcast capital. The crowd appeared blissful despite the clouds. The world was passing him by.

'Kieran?!' Nathan raised his voice as they approached a set of traffic lights.

'Yes, I've got it.'

'Good, and I want you to give that therapist a ring – Vivian Moses. We've used her before, and she's got availability after your photo call.'

Kieran frowned. 'What photo call?'

'For God's sake, don't tell me you've forgotten already,' Nathan replied as the lights changed to green. 'After your first training session.'

'Fucking hell, I just want to train without a fuss.'

'Kieran,' Nathan said, adopting the patronising tone that he disliked. The sound his voice took on when he wasn't getting his way. The way he spoke when he was attempting to disguise his growing frustration by coaxing his star client. 'You know what the deal is. It'll all be worth it.'

'Yeah,' Kieran replied unconvincingly.

FREDDIE, 2011

'We pray for peace. We pray for unity. We must come together because we know that we cannot do this on our own.'

Freddie listened to the pastor's voice reverberating through the speakerphone, his African accent loud and clear. 'Whether you are black or white, Muslim or Christian, we gather here today with the same goal – to pray for our community that is hurting.' The crowd cheered in agreement.

Freddie looked around at the hundreds gathered, eyes closed and heads bowed. He thought about how through the tragedy of Devon Constance's shooting, these people were united. The sea of faces were predominantly black, but there were white people too. Young and old, male and female.

Freddie bowed his head as the pastor continued to speak. He thought about how it didn't have to be like this. He quietly asked himself why it took such heartbreak to bring people together.

As a montage of burning buildings and upturned vehicles, looters running through Woundham high street with trolleys full of stolen goods, and riot police and members of the public violently clashing played in his head, Freddie tried to take comfort in the fact that only four days ago peace of any sort seemed impossible.

Despite the togetherness of this afternoon's vigil, Freddie felt like an outsider. He had decided against his wife, Carol, attending the vigil with him.

He shuddered at the thought of the verbal abuse that could have come his and his Caucasian spouse's way. He had secretly feared that this abuse could even be physical. So far, today's gathering had gone without incident; the heavy police presence seemingly having an effect.

'... Lord in your mercy, hear our prayer.' The crowd erupted into applause as the pastor's intercession came to an end.

Freddie looked up and joined in the applause. 'Amen,' he said as he crossed himself. It was then that Freddie felt a sharp pain at the back of his head. He heard someone cry out, and the crowd heaved and jostled as he fell to the ground.

Freddie cradled himself on his hands and knees, feeling around for his missing spectacles. He narrowed his eyes, desperately trying and failing to get to his feet.

'No ... please. In the Lord's name I ask for calm!' Freddie heard the pastor scream. He tried to look up but without his glasses his vision was blurry. All he could see were knees rushing about, one of them almost catching him on his temple. He felt the back of his head and knew that the warm liquid on his hands was blood. As the pain became sharper his vision became blurrier.

'Calm, please!' the pastor's African voice boomed.

Freddie was still on his hands and knees. He wasn't sure, but just before it went dark, he thought he heard somebody whisper 'sellout' in his ear.

KIERAN, TUESDAY 3 P.M.

'When I'm on the pitch, nothing else matters. When I score a goal, I feel invincible. Recognition from my teammates, tens of thousands of people chanting my name …' Kieran Ledley, the most expensive player in the history of the Premier League, paused to take a sip of water. 'It makes me feel as if I matter. And when the final whistle goes, the fear sets in.'

'What is the fear?' asked Vivian.

In keeping with his nature, Kieran continued to avoid eye contact with Vivian. 'The fear of going back to my real life.'

'Does the result of the match you've just played in make a difference to how you feel?'

'Not really,' Kieran replied, fidgeting with his ten thousand pound watch. 'I hate losing, but I hate leaving the pitch more. I'm nothing without football, and that scares me.'

Vivian looked down at her notes. 'You've been with Clarissa for eight years?'

Kieran didn't respond.

Vivian paused before continuing. 'That's a long time to be in a relationship with somebody, especially since you are twenty-four years old.'

Kieran simply took a deep breath.

Vivian smiled. 'How do you feel about going home to your fiancée after a game?'

'I don't know … I'm kinda used to her not being there. Touring, or whatever.'

Vivian waited for Kieran to continue before asking, 'Are you proud of Clarissa? Of her music career?'

Kieran shrugged his shoulders. There was silence until he said, 'I just need the high of my game all the time. I don't care about the money, or the fame. The only thing the money is good for is the power.'

'How would you define power?'

Kieran watched Vivian write in her file. 'I would describe power as the ability to make yourself feel the way you want to feel.'

Kieran took a sip from his glass of water. He replaced it on the table, the sound of glass connecting with glass interrupting the silence that had fallen on the room.

Kieran cleared his throat. 'You're waiting for me to say "Women, drugs – that's how I make myself feel good."'

Vivian regarded Kieran with a pleasant smile. 'Whatever it is, it's substitution. Replacing one high with another. Nothing in excess is good for you, Kieran.'

Kieran took a rare look into Vivian's eyes. 'So I've heard.' Suddenly self-conscious, he looked away.

'You can't live on the pitch forever, Kieran.'

NATHAN

The screen illuminated Nathan's large face as he sat hunched over his laptop. He mopped his sweaty brow, trying to figure out how to win back the three thousand pounds he'd just lost. Nathan had only recently cleared the twenty-seven thousand pound gambling debt he had fallen into. His ten per cent of Kieran's signing-on fee had come in very handy, but the pattern was beginning to repeat itself, and he knew it.

Nathan would take Kieran to horse races and justify his 'little punts here and there' by saying it was research. He would tell Kieran that it was all an investment, that he was looking after their interests outside the game, that they could consider buying the horse if it won. And if the football player attempted to argue, Nathan would retort, 'Footy is a short career. Trust me. I've never let you down, have I?'

This rhetorical question would be followed by a condescending fatherly pat on Kieran's cheek and, depending on the outcome of the race, a cheer or a groan.

Nathan didn't have an excuse for his online poker addiction.

Whenever he lost money he would remind himself that his biggest win was almost fifty thousand pounds. This was against his biggest loss of thirty-eight thousand, so as far as he was concerned he was in profit. Besides, what else was he supposed to do? He worked hard to protect Kieran and keep him happy. He needed to reward himself from time to time. Maybe if his wife hadn't left him eleven years ago he would have better things to occupy his evenings with. Perhaps if next week he was going to be celebrating his only son's twenty-sixth birthday, rather than the seventeenth anniversary of his tragic drowning, he wouldn't be sitting in his lonely penthouse telling himself that 'life is a gamble.'

The light from the screen slowly flickered and danced across Nathan's expression. He squinted. 'Fuck it,' he mumbled as he pressed the buttons on his keyboard. 'Fifteen thousand all in.'

FREDDIE, 2011

'Daddy!' Theo, Freddie's nine-year-old son ran towards him.

'Hello champ,' Freddie said as they embraced. Propped up in the hospital bed, he looked at his wife, who was holding Alfie, their five-year-old.

With a more sombre expression, Carol took in the sight of her husband's heavily bandaged head. 'Oh honey,' she said as she walked over and kissed him on the lips.

'Are you guys okay?' Freddie asked.

'We're fine. It's you that's got us panicking, for goodness sake.' She examined Freddie's head before touching the bandage. 'Oh darling,' she sighed as Freddie winced.

He took Alfie from Carol and gave him a kiss.

'Freddie, this is ridiculous. Police outside your ward—'

'I told them that I don't remember much—' Freddie interrupted.

'It's getting out of hand now—' Carol cut back in.

'I didn't manage to get a good look at them—'

'Freddie. Listen to me!' Carol shouted, annoyed at their overlapping conversation.

Freddie stopped talking.

A momentary silence fell upon the private ward. Carol looked at her husband's chastened features, his mouth hanging slightly open. She saw Theo and Alfie staring at her with their large, confused eyes.

A middle-aged nurse entered the ward.

Sensing the tension in the room, she said, 'Would you like me to take the kids to the play area?'

Carol turned to her. 'Errm …'

'Don't worry,' the nurse said with a reassuring smile, 'it's just down the corridor, they'll be fine.'

Carol looked at the two police officers chatting through the window.

'Go with the nice nurse, boys,' Freddie said, kissing Alfie on the forehead. He handed him over to the nurse. 'Go on, it's okay,' he said, turning to Theo.

Carol smiled at her apprehensive sons. 'I'll be there in a moment … Thank you,' she said as the nurse led the boys out of the ward.

Carol sat on the chair beside Freddie's bed. 'Darling, I'm scared.' She took his hands in hers. 'Please, I want you to pull back a bit.'

Freddie exhaled slowly. 'What does that mean?'

'It means that this isn't worth risking your life over.'

'Carol, I can't abandon these people. This is my job. Please do not exaggerate – I am not risking my life.'

Carol let go of her husband's hands and stood up. 'You were attacked, for crying out loud!'

'Keep your voice down,' Freddie said through gritted teeth.

'No!' Carol shouted.

'Carol,' Freddie appealed, glancing towards the door where he could see the two officers looking in their direction.

'Stop pretending, Freddie,' Carol continued. 'I'm sick and tired of this. You were attacked. Do any of "these people" care about that?'

Freddie raised a hand. 'Hang on a second … what do you mean by "these people?"'

'What?' Carol asked, adjusting her green cardigan.

'You heard me. What did you mean by that?'

Carol could sense his anger. 'Stop being silly, you know I didn't mean it in that way.'

'In what way?' Freddie asked, straightening his black-rimmed spectacles and fixing his wife with a penetrating gaze.

Carol flicked one side of her brunette bob behind her ear. 'Don't you dare,' she said. 'Don't you dare suggest that.'

Freddie gave her a cold stare and shrugged.

'So I'll never understand what it is to be black,' Carol said, trembling with emotion. 'It's not my fault that I wasn't born a black man. You know I support and love you. But before you continue trying to prove yourself to people, think about your family.'

Freddie lay back on the bed.

Carol took a step towards him. 'Are you listening to me? Think about our sons.'

As Freddie conjured up an image of tall thin Theo and small chubby Alfie, his beautiful brown boys with matching short Afros just like his own, a tear rolled from his eye to his ear before disappearing into his bandage.

RUPAL, MONDAY 11 A.M.

'I know little old me wouldn't have made a difference, but watching the riots on TV, I thought, yeah, you fuckers, you deal with it.' Rupal began to nod as she stared past Vivian. 'It's like, I'm an ethnic minority so I'm a sellout for being a policewoman, but at the same time I'm not treated the same as my white and male colleagues in the force, so fuck it. I'm angry too.'

Vivian wrote in her file and then looked up at Rupal.

Rupal's small shoulders heaved as she breathed a deep sigh of relief. 'It feels nice to get that off my chest.' She took a sip of water.

'So you don't feel any sympathy towards your former colleagues about the difficult and dangerous situation the London riots put them in?' Vivian asked.

Rupal pulled the sleeves of her black cardigan over her small hands and briefly shut her eyes, which Vivian observed were slightly bloodshot.

'That's the thing ... of course I do. But there was also a sense of satisfaction ...' Rupal looked at Vivian as if silently urging her to fill in the blanks. The silence continued until Rupal said, 'You see, sick isn't it?'

Vivian didn't speak.

'I'm lost.' Rupal continued. 'How can I think like this? I'm so bitter about my experience with the Met that I'm confused.'

'What do you mean?' Vivian asked.

Rupal puffed her cheeks, seeming irritated by Vivian's question. 'I'm confused about who I am. Less than five years ago there's no way that I would have left any space for the justification of looting, or of rioting. And I definitely wouldn't have stood for any violence against the police.' Rupal bit her bottom lip and adjusted her thick black ponytail. 'It completely goes against everything I believed in.'

'Do you keep in touch with any of your former colleagues?'

Rupal shook her head. 'I've deleted all their numbers. None of them were there for me when we worked together, so I don't expect to go for a drink with any of them now.'

'What about the other females you worked with? Do you feel they could have looked after—'

Rupal held both hands up. 'Excuse me, I don't need looking after by anybody.'

Vivian pursed her lips. 'I see.' After a pause Vivian asked, 'And what about them, have any of your colleagues tried to keep in contact with you?'

Rupal looked towards the carpet and started to blink continuously, each flap of her eyelids bringing up tears. 'Nikesh.'

Vivian reached over to her desk and placed a box of tissues in front of her patient.

'Thanks,' Rupal said as she grabbed a handful. 'PC Nikesh.'

Vivian was a little surprised when she heard a slight chuckle come from Rupal. 'In my head that stood for 'Politically Correct' Nikesh.'

Vivian smiled.

'At first,' Rupal continued, 'it was that weird thing of "just because we're both Indian, it doesn't mean we have to be friends."'

'Ah,' Vivian nodded with a relaxed smile, 'the unspoken "ethnic blanking".'

'Yeah,' Rupal said in a tone that suggested she was surprised by Vivian's understanding. She continued to look at Vivian who, still wearing the smile, leaned back into her sofa and folded her arms.

'We eventually became alright with each other,' Rupal went on. 'I was impressed by the way he seemed comfortable with everyone.' She took a sip of water. 'But one evening after a shift, a few of us were at the pub and some of the guys started making racist jokes. It was so uncomfortable and he did nothing. He just sat there and let me be the one to tell them that they were being inappropriate.'

Rupal paused and looked at Vivian, who smiled sympathetically.

'So from then on I was known as the uptight cow with a chip on my shoulder. How is that fair?'

Vivian topped up both their glasses with water. 'It's not.'

'Exactly,' Rupal replied, 'it's not fair.' She drank from her glass. 'I confronted him about it the next day at work but he said that it wasn't a big deal and that I should pick my battles. How fucking dare he?' Rupal scanned Vivian's face attempting to gauge whether her therapist shared her incredulity. 'He's texted me a few times since I left but I lost all respect for him after that.'

'That's understandable,' Vivian replied.

Rupal's eyes began to well up again. 'So you see. I'm bitter, angry and unemployed.'

DAILY REFLECTION
Tuesday, 27th September, 2011

HE SHOOTS, AND SCORES!

'My all night bash with footy superstar.'

An aspiring glamour model has told of her seedy night of booze and sex with the world's most expensive football player, Kieran Ledley.

Last night, Jodie K, from North London, told how she was 'picked up' by the star last week at the trendy nightspot, Whispers, in Central London.

The 26-year-old model said, 'I was at the club with a girlfriend, and we were at the bar drinking and laughing at all the females trying to get the attention of some of the celebrities in the venue.

'I had heard that Kieran was going to be there celebrating with some of his teammates after their victory. As soon as he walked in you could see the attention shift towards him and his entourage. He was with about seven guys. I recognised some of them as football players. They were led to the VIP area by two large security guards, and just before Kieran disappeared behind the velvet ropes, our eyes met. It was only a brief moment, but it was clear that he was interested in me.'

What Jodie told us next is sure to send shockwaves through the pop world too, as his fiancée, 24-year-old Clarissa Harvey, lead singer of the group Girl-

Fiends, has been recently seen wearing her £1.2 million engagement ring again, after calling off their pending nuptials earlier this year following a string of allegations over Ledley's infidelity.

'I knew it was only a matter of time before someone would send for me on Kieran's behalf. About ten minutes later, an older guy, who I now know is his agent, approached me and my girlfriend at the bar. At first I thought he was some sleazy businessman trying to crack on to me.

'But then he told me he was a friend of Kieran Ledley, and that he wanted to offer us a "cool, carefree night."

'Me and my friend were up for it. We thought: why not? She's just split up from her long-term boyfriend, and I don't do relationships.

'We followed the older guy to the VIP area, and Kieran was sitting on a sofa surrounded by some of his friends and teammates drinking expensive champagne. He smiled and waved me over.'

The busty brunette went on. 'Even though I've been with a few famous faces in the past, I was quite excited at the prospect of spending some time with the world's most expensive football player. I'm not really into the sport, but everyone knows Kieran Ledley.

'His pal made room for me and I sat down. After pouring me a glass of champagne, the first thing Kieran said to me was, "Have we had sex before?" I was slightly taken aback by his forward question, so I giggled and said no. He just smiled at me and said, "Well, we need to do something about that."

'There were quite a few people in the room – guys and girls hanging out with each other – and most of them just carried on with their drinking and talking, although thinking back to it now, I was getting some envious looks from a couple of girls there. Kieran said he'd be back in a minute and then went to have a word with his agent.

'While he was gone I turned to my girlfriend, who was busy talking to somebody I recognised. I'm not sure but I think he was an actor or a TV presenter.

'Kieran came back and said that there was a car waiting for us outside. I smiled and said okay.

'The next few hours were a blur. One minute we were talking in the club, then we were sneaked out of the back door into a 4x4, and then into the Summit Hotel in Hyde Park.'

It was there where Jodie had sex with Ledley, 24. Suites at the hotel start from £3,000 a night.

'The whole thing was like some sort of military operation. He's the most secretive of any celebrity I've been with, but I guess it's because he's involved with Clarissa Harvey.'

Asked whether she felt guilty that she was about to have sex with the fiancé of one of the country's most famous singers, Jodie replied, 'Not really. I mean, as a woman, it would be awful to have that happen to you, but at the end of the day, Kieran's a grown man, and he makes his own decisions. Besides, I'm not the one in a relationship, he is.'

When asked if she herself had ever been cheated on, Jodie said, 'Not to my knowledge, but that's because I don't really do relationships, and if I did [do relationships], I'd like to think that I'd satisfy them enough to prevent them going elsewhere.'

Jodie says they had sex twice.

'Kieran's agent had been in the car with us, and I told him that I hoped his friend wasn't expecting a threesome! Kieran laughed, and said that I shouldn't worry, and that he was only there to make sure that we got to the hotel okay.

'Kieran's agent went through the front of the hotel, and me and Kieran went in through a fire exit. An enormous bodyguard met us there, walked us to the lift, and led us to a room on the twelfth floor.

'My heart was pounding with excitement at the espionage nature of it all, and I cheekily whispered to Kieran that I hoped it was all going to be worth it! He gave me a cocky smile and just put his fingers to his lips.

'The bodyguard led us to the door, and me and Kieran entered the room. The suite was amazing and had a beautiful view all across London. Standing at the window, looking out at the city, I was feeling very sexy. Kieran came up behind me and started to remove my dress.

'He was confident and very gentle, surprisingly gentle considering that this was about to be a one-night stand. Within minutes we were both naked. I performed oral sex on him and we had sex for about twenty minutes. He was a lot slimmer than I thought he would be, and perhaps a little shorter. I knew he was fit, but he always looked a little bigger on TV and in the papers. He was also well endowed. Not overly big, but I would say above average. And he certainly knew what he was doing.

'When we finished our first session, he lay there staring at the ceiling. It was clear that something was on his mind. I was going to ask him if he felt guilty, but I thought that there wasn't any point, and I personally didn't want to ruin the good time we'd both been having. We drank and chatted a little bit before performing oral sex on each other.

'We had sex again and he was a little more aggressive this time, and was keen to try different positions.

'I woke up around 7.30 a.m., so we had only had around four hours sleep, but he was wide awake and fully clothed. This surprised me a little because I knew that he had just played a full match the day before. Add this to the time we had together, and it was amazing that he still seemed to have more energy left.

'He told me that there was a car waiting for me downstairs. His agent came in and said he would walk me over. I said that I wanted to have a shower first but his agent looked irritated and said, "There isn't any time, babe."

'I wasn't too happy about this but wrote my number on a scrap piece of paper and handed it to Kieran. I could see that he didn't really like the way his agent spoke to me either. Even though he's very cocky on the pitch, and he often has all sorts written about him, he's actually quite sweet. We kissed and then I left the room.'

On whether she thinks they'll ever see each other again, Jodie says, 'He's got my number, so who knows?'

KIERAN, WEDNESDAY 5 P.M.

'I just want to remind you, Kieran, everything you say in this room is strictly confidential.'

Kieran drank from the glass Vivian had just poured for him. He shut his eyes tightly and ran a hand over his short, curly, dark-brown hair. 'Thanks for fitting me in at such short notice.'

Vivian nodded. 'That's absolutely fine.'

'I'm gutted about the story.' He zipped his tracksuit all the way up to his hairless chin and pulled at the collar as if trying to hide his face.

'Have you heard from Clarissa?' Vivian asked.

Kieran shook his head, the diamond studs in each ear catching the light. 'No. Not since she moved out again.'

'Do you know where she's gone?'

Kieran sighed. 'Probably to her mum's again.'

Vivian sat back on her couch and rolled her pen between her thumb and index finger. 'Again?'

Kieran looked up, confused. 'Huh?'

'You just said "again" twice,' Vivian replied.

'Yeah … that's what happened last time.'

'Last time you had a fight, or the last time a story was written about you?'

Kieran pursed his lips and looked down at the carpet.

'You said it very casually both times.' Vivian placed the pen on the coffee table in front of her. 'This is clearly a recurring theme, isn't it Kieran? What are the stakes?'

Kieran continued to look towards the ground. 'I only want to be judged on the pitch.'

'You are an incredibly famous man, Kieran,' Vivian said, sitting up. 'People are judgemental by nature. People are even more judgemental of those who they perceive to be in a privileged position.'

Kieran locked eyes with his therapist. 'I'm not "privileged". I've worked my nuts off for everything I have.'

Vivian nodded. 'No doubt. But people only see the end result. Stories like the one in the paper the other day only give them more ammunition to judge you.'

'Yeah, but … it's so hard. What am I supposed to do? Sit at home all evening so things aren't written about me? These people think that they own me. The chairman, the manager, even the fans. I don't owe any of them anything but a good performance.'

Kieran began to feel uncomfortably warm as Vivian held his gaze. He unzipped his tracksuit and cast his eyes away.

'And what about Clarissa?' Vivian asked.

Kieran sipped his water.

'Do you owe her anything?'

Kieran met Vivian's question with silence.

'After all,' Vivian continued, 'she is your fiancée. A young woman who I expect has also worked hard to be in the position she's in.'

'I didn't mean to embarrass ... I never meant to ...'

Vivian leaned forward. 'You're right, Kieran. People are very quick to judge. But you have to ask yourself – what are the stakes?'

'I don't ... I don't understand.' Kieran replied.

'Perhaps because Clarissa has forgiven you in the past the stakes aren't high enough. Perhaps you don't think you'll ever lose her. Maybe you think you're invincible.'

There was a pause before Kieran fixed his eyes on Vivian's. 'I don't think I'm invincible. I'm scared.'

GEMMA AND PETE, WEDNESDAY 6 P.M.

'What kind of man doesn't give a fuck what his wife gets up to?!'

Pete rubbed his eyes and kept his face in his hands. 'Stop,' he requested in a tiny voice.

Vivian looked at her watch and then glanced towards the door. 'Guys, I'm sorry but we've gone nearly ten minutes over—'

Gemma turned to Vivian. 'Can you imagine being with a man that doesn't care if another male tries to chat you up in front of him?'

Pete let out a long sigh. 'What are you talking about?'

'There you go,' Gemma said as she stood over her husband. 'Completely oblivious!'

Pete sighed again as he ran his palms over his face. Vivian then turned her attention back to the panting Gemma, while doing her best to remain unruffled by her unruly patient.

'Right in front of your eyes, that pop star fella.' Gemma put her hands on her hips as she looked between Pete and Vivian expectantly.

Pete sighed again. 'What pop star fella? What are you talking about, you crazy woman?'

'Right, guys,' Vivian said, remaining in her seat, 'I'm really going to have to ask the both of you to leave now—'

'You fucking blind bat! The one married to that Clarissa Harvey!' Gemma shouted.

'Gemma—'

'The guy that we saw in the car park on our way in!' Gemma bellowed over Vivian. 'Getting into his Ferrari or whatever it was!'

'Okay, Gemma,' Vivian said, now raising her voice. 'That is another patient—'

Pete threw his head back and looked towards the ceiling, 'Oh for fuck's sake.'

'Ahh, now you remember?' A twisted smile began to form on Gemma's face. 'Maybe I'm not so crazy after all.'

Vivian observed Pete bite his bottom lip and focus on the carpet. His shoulders appeared to be trembling slightly. He said, 'He's a football player.'

Gemma appeared momentarily confused and Vivian quickly raised a hand towards her before she could respond. 'That really is enough now.'

She was speaking fast, half expecting another interruption. 'We do not discuss other patients in this room—'

'Whatever he is!' Gemma's interruption arrived. 'He was eyeing me up right in front of you, and you did nothing!'

Pete refused to look at his wife. 'You really better stop shouting at me.'

Gemma waved both her arms dramatically. 'Oh, you're making threats now are you?'

'Gemma, if you continue to behave like this I do not think that—'

Gemma ignored Vivian and continued to goad her husband. 'Why don't you go and threaten that pop guy, then? For all you know this has been going on for ages. Maybe he and I have been getting to know each other all this time.'

Pete clenched his fists.

'Maybe the eyes he was giving me is our secret code. Are you going to let somebody disrespect you like that? At a place where we're all supposed to be getting help?!'

Pete turned to Vivian. 'Did you know anything about this?'

Vivian was caught off guard. 'What?'

'Did you?'

'No!' Vivian composed herself and lowered her tone. 'I think this is completely … that was a rearranged session.'

Pete's voice was no longer tiny. 'I'm tired of all the lies, and ridicule …'

Vivian took in the dysfunctional couple. She was exhausted and simply wanted them out of her sight.

With her judgement perhaps clouded by fatigue, the only way she felt she could bring the situation under control was by saying, 'Gemma, there is no way your paths could have previously crossed here as that appointment was rescheduled from a Tuesday.'

Gemma and Pete stared at their therapist.

Knowing she had said too much, Vivian sighed before saying to Pete, 'Look, even if I did know anything, I would have to respect patient confidentiality.'

Gemma snorted.

Vivian looked at the desperate woman. 'Gemma,' she began, using every ounce of calm she could, 'what are you trying to achieve?'

'I'm trying to wake this pussy up! I'm trying to find out what kind of man he considers himself to be. Let me help you out, Pete!' Gemma screamed in an octave that Vivian was unsure any patient of hers had ever reached. 'You're a weak, selfish man. You're not even a man … you're a boy!'

In an instant Pete jumped to his feet and grabbed Gemma by the throat. 'Stop, just stop!' he hissed through gritted teeth.

Vivian leapt up and placed her hands on Pete's thick shoulders. 'Pete, please.'

Gemma struggled to breathe as she attempted to remove Pete's hands from her neck. 'That's better, that's what I want to see,' she shouted as she looked into her husband's wide eyes and saw something she hadn't seen for years. 'Finally, some passion!'

Pete pushed her towards the sofa and Gemma let herself fall onto it.

'Is this what you want?' Pete asked Gemma. His shoulders were heaving and he wore an expression more menacing than Gemma had ever seen him possess.

Gemma rubbed her sore neck and stared up at him, momentarily speechless.

Pete turned towards Vivian. He adjusted his rumpled blue shirt, wiped the saliva from around his mouth and said, 'I'm sorry.' He looked at his watch. 'I'll pay you for the extra time.' Pete patted his pockets as if he was searching for his wallet, then left the room.

Vivian looked at Gemma on the sofa. 'Are you okay?' she asked.

Gemma continued to rub her neck. 'How is he going to pay for anything if he hasn't got any money?'

Vivian frowned.

Gemma was still rubbing her neck. 'Wow,' she said in a quiet voice. 'Wow.'

NATHAN

'Fuck!' Nathan shouted as he exited the bookies and walked towards his black Range Rover. There was a yellow parking fine on the windscreen. He jogged up to the traffic warden who was now taking down the details of another vehicle further up the road. 'Come on, mate,' Nathan panted. 'I can't have been more than a couple of minutes late. You can see I paid to park.'

'Sorry,' the warden replied in an African accent. 'Appeal to the council but you won't win.' He continued to take down the details of the car in front of him.

'You fucking bastard!' Nathan screamed, causing a lady who was passing by with a small girl to glare at him. 'Sorry,' he called after the woman, who didn't look back. He followed the warden who was now moving off. 'Why don't you get a proper job, you piece of shit?!'

The warden squared up to Nathan and they looked at each other for the first time: Nathan, overweight and sweaty in his grey suit; the warden, black, shiny skin, early thirties, in an oversized green uniform. He removed his hat revealing his even shinier scalp. 'What did just you call me?'

Nathan blinked and suddenly found he couldn't respond.

'This is a proper job.' The African traffic warden pointed towards Nathan's Range Rover. 'If you can afford a nice car like that you should have been able to put more money in the meter. Now walk away from me before I slap you.'

Nathan was so stunned by the even-tempered tone in which this was delivered that he found himself muttering an involuntary apology. 'Sorry … I've just had a bad … day.'

By the time Nathan had finished speaking, the warden was further up the road inspecting other vehicles. Nathan walked back over to his car and removed the parking ticket. He threw a disgusted look towards the bookies and sat in the driver's seat. Nathan loosened his navy tie and rested his forehead on the steering wheel, trying to figure out how he had just lost sixty thousand pounds.

VIVIAN

Domestic violence is a very strange thing. There's the obvious physical pain that follows, but then there's also the mental scarring it leaves you with. Women especially ask themselves if it's their fault. Was it me that pushed him to hit me? I certainly asked myself that question. I'd sit at my kitchen table crying into a bottle of vodka wondering if I deserved this abuse because of my drinking problem. I wondered if perhaps I disgusted my husband so much that he had no choice but to hit me, to beat my pathetic dependency out of me. I'd then empty my cabinets of all the spirits I had and pour them down the sink, promising myself that this was it, that I'd be dry from that moment on. Then I'd replace my alcohol addiction with the obsession of getting my husband onside. I'd spend the next four days hell-bent on making him love me again. Four days was normally the most I could handle. In that period my husband and I would have a fight that would end up with me on the floor after another violent beating from him. He'd leave the house and slam the door behind him as I lay there, thinking about how embarrassed I was to talk to anybody about this recurring theme. I knew my friends would simply tell me to leave him, and that my parents would echo this, and tell me to contact the police. I also knew that they'd be surprised that I was a victim. Not strong, ambitious Vivian Moses. It took me a long time to realise that it was my husband's feelings of inadequacy that made him beat me. We had been unsuccessfully trying for a baby for almost three years, and after spending the majority of that time blaming myself, we found out that he was infertile.

We spoke about adoption but he decided that he couldn't bring himself to love a child without any resentment that we hadn't conceived naturally. The night when we were in bed and he cried into my arms, declaring himself a failure, was the moment I lost the man I fell in love with. Less than two years into our marriage he left his highly paid job as a graphic designer to set up his own company. The company never took off. I prayed that something would come in for him. I prayed that we'd be able to have a baby, and most of all I promised myself that I would do everything I could to not emasculate him.

What I witnessed in my last session with Gemma and Pete angered me deeply. The sight of a man putting his hands on a woman in such a way disgusts me. But I couldn't help thinking about Gemma's behaviour. It's clear that she has been pushing Pete's buttons. My violent marriage made me become fascinated in human emotions. Why do people behave the way they do? After my husband was locked up, I vowed to never make excuses for domestic violence again. Abuse is abuse.

And although in Gemma and Pete's case violence is not what brought them to be patients of mine, in our last session, who was the abuser and who was the victim? Fascinating.

There was a knock at the door. Vivian stopped writing and looked up. She put her pen on her desk. 'Just a moment,' she called. She placed her file in her desk drawer and fished out another one.

Adjusting her dark-purple blazer and straightening her black pencil skirt, Vivian walked over to her couch and sat down. 'Come in,' she called towards the door.

In walked Rupal.

RUPAL, MONDAY 11 A.M.

'My boyfriend, George, he just doesn't seem to understand me. I mean he tries, bless him. But he'll never be Indian, will he?'

Vivian crossed her legs and smiled at Rupal.

'He says things like "It doesn't matter what people say" and it's like, "Honey, you just don't get it".'

'Are you angry with his attitude towards your feelings?'

'Well, yes,' Rupal replied after offering a confused look to Vivian. 'Wouldn't you be? It's as if he thinks that I should just get on with it. As if I should be happy that I'm with an open-minded English bloke. Well, sorry mate, I'm not after your approval.'

'I see.' Vivian nodded her head slowly. 'So you think that he feels you should be grateful that you're with somebody outside of your community?'

Rupal suddenly appeared very sad. 'Yes I do, actually. And I hate it. That's exactly the way I used to feel at work. "Shut up and deal with it, little Indian girl. We let you in." I'm sick of it.' Rupal's eyes welled up, and she looked like a small child on the couch.

Vivian went over to her desk behind her and returned with a box of tissues.

'Thank you,' Rupal said as she dabbed the corner of her eyes. She curled her legs up onto the sofa, her petite frame now appearing even tinier. 'George has this friend, Daniel. He's a wealthy black guy. And he's so fucking arrogant. He's always bleating on about people trying to take down the black man, blah, blah, blah. It's like – sorry mate, but no. You've got money. It's a man's world, shut up. Do you know what I mean? I say it to George all the time but he worships the bloody guy.' Rupal scrunched the tissue into a ball. 'You should hear him complain. I'm sorry but it's not the blacks that have it the worst anymore. No disrespect, Vivian.'

FREDDIE, THURSDAY 1 P.M.

Freddie sipped his water. 'Maybe if I thought more like my sister, things would be different.'

Vivian crossed her legs and adjusted her red skirt. 'What do you mean by that?'

'My sister, Chioma, doesn't agree with interracial relationships.'

'I see.' Vivian made a note then rested her file on her thighs. She watched Freddie lean back on the sofa and touch the back of his head. 'How is it?' she asked.

Freddie furrowed his brows, as if momentarily confused.

Vivian then made a striking gesture and gave a sympathetic smile. 'Your head?'

'Oh,' Freddie replied, managing a smile back. 'It's getting better.'

Vivian nodded.

'Chioma never came to our wedding.'

'Because Carol is white?'

Freddie pushed his glasses further up his nose and shrugged.

After writing something down, Vivian said, 'Maybe Chioma took this as a rejection of herself.'

Freddie squinted, looking intrigued, at Vivian.

'Carol looks nothing like her. Perhaps she sees it as you confirming that someone like her can't be loved.'

Freddie rubbed his chin, his gaze now extending beyond Vivian.

Seeing the bewilderment etched on Freddie's face, Vivian continued, 'You're her older brother. After your father left, you became somewhat of a father-figure to her.' Vivian flicked through her notes. 'You said that when you left to go to university, your relationship with your sister broke down ...'

'Yes, maybe I could have kept in touch with her a little more during that period.'

'Maybe, but you were young,' Vivian said softly. 'You were on an adventure. You can't blame yourself too much. It's possible that she saw that period as you abandoning her just as your father did.' Vivian paused, and when Freddie simply stared at her, she continued, 'And she could have taken marrying a white woman as confirmation of the "rejection".'

'I didn't mean to ...' Freddie struggled. 'My mother was okay with it. I would never reject ...'

'You didn't reject anyone, Freddie. You must stop blaming yourself.'

Freddie looked down at his near empty glass of water. Vivian topped it up.

'Thank you,' he said, taking a sip. 'But maybe Chioma's right. Carol doesn't understand what it's like. It's almost as if I've made things harder for myself.'

Vivian pursed her lips. 'How do you mean?'

'I knew I wouldn't be able to bring my wife to the vigil with me last week. I would have been crucified.' He looked up at Vivian. 'What kind of bullshit burden is that to carry around?'

Vivian cleared her throat but didn't reply.

'There was a heavy police presence there that day but I was still attacked.' Antipathy was now the prevalent tone in Freddie's voice. 'They probably saw the assailant coming towards me,' Freddie continued bitterly, 'and they probably thought, "Let them all continue to hurt each other."' Freddie looked at Vivian and he seemed annoyed when she opted to jot something down instead of coming up with some sort of answer. 'Hang on a second, Vivian.'

She looked up.

'Do you hear what I'm saying?'

'Yes,' Vivian replied.

'So you can see how I'm stuck? That I'm a "sellout" according to the people in my constituency, but I'm still a "black man" in the eyes of the law?'

Vivian studied Freddie, silently.

'Do you understand me? Can you see that I'm trapped in identity purgatory?' Freddie's question was awash with resentment. 'The people of Woundham, let alone the black community, don't see me as black. But I still suffer the same prejudices as they do.'

Freddie shook his head and once again fixed his gaze beyond Vivian. 'Why can't they see that? We are the same … we're the same.'

Vivian spoke. 'Freddie. We are all the same in that we are a product of our environment. It is that environment that makes us see things differently. The more you remember that, the easier it is to accept that you cannot fight everyone's battles.'

'But I want to make a difference—'

'You are,' Vivian reassured him.

'No,' Freddie said with a defeated expression. 'I thought I was, but I'm not.' He shook his head. 'I can't even get them to see that destroying their own neighbourhood is not the answer. Devon Constance's death is being lost in all of this, and that's not right.' Freddie sipped from his glass. He removed his spectacles and wiped them on his grey shirt. 'Obama,' he said, as he put them back on.

'What about him?' Vivian asked with a slight frown.

'My kids are mixed race but the world sees them as black.' Freddie smiled ruefully, 'The "one drop rule".'

Vivian smiled back. 'A little bit of black and you're black.'

Freddie nodded. 'As if they've been infected.'

'Wouldn't you say that's more of an American way of thinking—?'

'I don't know,' Freddie interrupted. 'Barack Obama is mixed but the world sees him as black, too. It seems many African Americans see him as one of their own. But me, I *am* black but not black enough for Woundham.'

Vivian put her file down. 'There is a thin line between being driven and having an unhealthy desire to prove ourselves.'

Freddie looked up at Vivian. 'My wife said something like that the other day.'

'Well,' Vivian smiled, 'your wife sounds like an intelligent woman.' Vivian let that hang in the air before saying, 'You're good enough for your wife, and you're good enough for your children. Crusades can drive a wedge between us and those that love us.'

Freddie replied with a silent stare.

'Have you ever thought about it from your wife's point of view? We all get judged.'

Freddie adjusted his spectacles.

'Have you ever spoken about how it was for Carol marrying a black man?'

'I mean ...' Freddie looked at Vivian patiently waiting for him to complete his sentence. 'There have been times ...'

'Either way,' Vivian said, 'we all have battles. We all judge and are the subject of judgement. You can't save the world, Freddie. But you can keep trying your best at your job. Overcompensating for marrying a white woman won't get you anywhere. Don't fall out with your wife for something that others may have an opinion on.'

Freddie nodded slowly.

'You have a beautiful family.'

'Thank you,' Freddie said. 'I don't want to lose them.'

'I don't see why you would,' Vivian replied reassuringly.

Freddie looked down at the carpet. 'I don't want to drive a wedge between us.'

Vivian watched him.

Freddie continued to stare at the carpet. 'I'll never leave my kids,' he said. 'I'll never leave them.'

VIVIAN

She let out short controlled breaths as she jogged up the steep hill. Wearing a cap to shield her eyes from the autumn sun, Vivian enjoyed the cool breeze slipping over her dark-brown skin. She let the music flowing from her headphones spur her on as she neared the summit. Smiling when she reached the top, she paused her digital watch and placed both hands on her slim thighs. With a deep breath she took in the sweeping views across the city. She could make out the arches of Wembley Stadium in the distance. Vivian looked up at the fleecy clouds drifting across the blue sky and shut her eyes. She reminisced about the times she used to do this run with her husband. Those days seemed so long ago, and though she had recently begun to acknowledge it, it took her a long time to admit that she missed it. Once a recreation that she and her husband bonded over, running was now an activity she used to escape. The effect of the endorphins was wearing off quicker after each arrival at the top of the hill, and it was when this high began to evaporate that she would ask herself what she was trying to escape from. Was it the misery of her patients' lives? Tales that would momentarily mask the fact that she had skeletons of her own? Was it, she wondered, an attempt to evade the temptation of drink?

Vivian placed her hands on her hips and continued to ask herself the questions she always did while looking out over North London and beyond from this vantage point. Questions that hitherto remained unanswered. Did she really enjoy helping people, or was it now a warped opportunity for her to tell herself that her life wasn't so bad? That she didn't need a man? That she hadn't alienated herself from her parents ever since the breakdown of her marriage? While running, and while talking to rowing couples, insecure athletes, and closet homosexuals, Vivian was able to forget that she was lonely.

Vivian removed her cap and ran a hand over her short hair. She felt a light raindrop as she began to stretch. She placed her cap back on her head and restarted her watch. As Vivian jogged back down the hill she came to terms with the fact that she still hadn't answered any of her own questions. But she knew there was something else she had to come to terms with.

PETE / KIERAN

'Bingo.'

Pete had been periodically resting his head on his dashboard for almost two hours. Staking out Vivian's car park was tiring. But the mental note he had made of Kieran's appointments had been worth it. He could see the football player getting into his car. 'Clueless bitch,' he muttered to himself, 'it's a Lamborghini.' Pete's palms became sweaty as he watched the fit young athlete put on his seatbelt. Startled by the roar of Kieran's engine, Pete turned the key in his own vehicle's ignition and sped into the path of Kieran's car before the football player could drive off. Pete broke sharply and Kieran lowered his window.

'What the fuck are you doing?' Kieran asked as he craned his neck out of his car.

Pete remained in his driver's seat, gripping the wheel.

Kieran undid his seatbelt. 'What the fuck?' he demanded again. He got out of his car and walked round to the front, inspecting his paintwork.

Pete looked at the much better looking, much younger man with glowing light-brown skin, standing there in his designer T-shirt, trendy jeans, and trainers so white they looked like they were being worn for the first time.

Kieran glanced around the car park before looking into Pete's car. He smiled sympathetically. 'It's okay, mate. There's no damage.'

Pete remained silent but began to pant.

'It's okay,' Kieran said again.

'No it's not,' Pete replied. He slowly got out of his car and saw Kieran look down at his expensive watch. 'You got somewhere to be?'

A look of confusion spread across Kieran's face.

Pete walked towards him. 'It's not okay.'

Kieran scanned the car park again, suspiciously this time. He took a step back as Pete approached. 'Look, mate ... I don't really know what your problem is—'

'My problem,' Pete hissed, 'is that it's not okay to fuck other people's wives!' He lunged at Kieran who swiftly leaned out of the way, causing Pete to fall to the ground.

Kieran stared down at the stranger sprawled on the concrete. 'Are you alright?'
Not knowing what to do, Kieran decided to help the man up.

'Get your hands off me!' The man shouted. He got to his feet, and after dusting
himself down he looked at Kieran. The two men stood in an awkward silence as
they stared at each other.

'Look ...' Kieran began. 'I don't know what to say ... who?'

'Pete ... it's Pete.' Pete shook his head. 'Unbelievable. You can have any girl
you want. Why my wife?'

'I think we should both go home and pretend that this never happened.' Kieran
cast his eyes around, just waiting for the lens of a camera to appear. He reached
for his car door.

'But it did happen, didn't it?' Pete said, his voice beginning to crack.

'I'm sorry,' Kieran replied. 'These girls, they just. They see a wealthy guy ... You
know what girls are like ... fuck ... I ...' Kieran felt like his tongue was tied into a
knot. He could feel adrenaline running through his body, but not his favourite kind.
This was nothing like scoring a goal, or being named man of the match. This was
... bizarre. He couldn't help thinking that he was being set up somehow. He came
to the conclusion that he really did need to get out of there so he got into his car.

'Exactly,' Pete said as he looked into Kieran's vehicle. 'Girls. Why are you
interested in a forty-year-old woman?'

Kieran furrowed his brow.

'That how you get your kicks is it?'

'Forty-year-old woman?'

Pete smiled. 'Gemma, Gemma.' He looked up to the grey sky and put his head in his hands. A stunned Kieran looked on as Pete laughed wickedly before looking up and asking, 'How old did my wife tell you she was?'

Kieran puffed his cheeks. 'Okay, I really don't know what's going on. I think maybe this is a dare or some sort of prank. But I don't know anybody called Gemma. I've never fucked a forty-year-old woman in my life—'

'Don't give me that crap—'

Before Pete finished his sentence Kieran began to reverse his car.

'Wait!' Pete shouted as he whipped his phone out of the back pocket of his corduroy trousers.

'What the fuck is this?' Kieran stared at Pete brandishing the phone. 'What are you doing? What do you want from me?'

Pete waved his mobile at Kieran. 'Do you know this woman?'

'Mate … Pete … whatever, can you please get the fuck away from me?'

Pete continued to wave his phone. 'Please just look! Do you know this fucking woman?!'

'Jesus Christ!' Kieran shouted.

'Look!' Pete shouted even louder.

Kieran reluctantly reached through his window and took the phone from Pete. He frowned as he looked at the screen and saw a picture of a smiling slim woman. 'Honestly, I have never seen this lady in my life.'

He handed the phone back to Pete.

There was a beat as Pete took his phone back and looked at his wife's happy expression. He couldn't remember when that photo had been taken. Not only could he not imagine being able to make her smile again, he wasn't sure he even wanted to. He closed his eyes and lowered his head. 'Sick bitch.'

Kieran put his car into gear. 'I'm going, and don't even think about following me, you nutter.' He stepped on the accelerator, and Pete watched Kieran's yellow Lamborghini disappear out of the car park.

GEMMA AND PETE, 1981

Gemma and Pete stared out over Harrow Viewpoint, and the stars blinked in the dark sky as Prince's *I Love U In Me* flowed from the cassette deck of Pete's navy, upgraded 1976 Hillman Avenger. It had been a lovely evening as far as the both of them were concerned. Pete had taken his new girlfriend out to dinner (it was the first time he had ever worn a blazer on a night out) to celebrate his new job as an editor's assistant. Gemma wasn't entirely sure what her boyfriend's job entailed, but she knew that he was now going to be spending his days working at a post-production facility in Soho. She also knew that Soho was a cool place where people wore bright clothes and always seemed to have coffees in their hands. And although she didn't want Pete's head to get big, she was very impressed.

Gemma had been taken aback by Pete's ambition the first night she met him at Carey Morgan's New Year's Eve party. While everyone was jumping on sofas dancing to Abba's *The Winner Takes It All,* Pete had homed in on the slim pretty girl with big brown hair. Gemma watched him confidently stroll over in his dark-green bomber jacket, fitted light-blue jeans, and crisp white Adidas shell toes. When he reached her standing by the messy table of scattered snacks, Pete told Gemma that he liked the biker jacket she was wearing. Gemma became shy and tried to mask this by acting cool and nodding in appreciation. Undeterred, Pete found out her name, that she was in her first year at uni, and that embarking on her English literature course back in October was her first time in London. 'But I'm from Bedford, which isn't that far away. So it's no big deal.'

Pete laughed, and made a joke about how some of the 'out of towners' he had met over the years at university (he was in his final few months) were always trying to play down London. Gemma was slightly irritated by this indirect accusation but she found herself laughing because Pete had put on some sort of lazy mocking voice when he said it. And that was it, ice broken. They dodged past the sweaty rocking bodies, went through to the kitchen and found a quieter spot. Pete opened a door which they found had some stairs on the other side that led down to the garden. A flustered looking couple stumbled up the last few stairs, which made Pete and Gemma jump. 'Sorry man,' the young, male, dark-haired student said to Pete as he adjusted his flies. Pete laughed and nodded as the young male squinted at him. 'Hey Pete! How's it going pal?'

The young man looked towards Gemma, then back to Pete. 'Ah,' a cheeky grin spread across the young man's face. 'I see!' He held out his hand for a high five, which Pete ignored. Gemma kept her satisfaction at Pete not partaking in the male bravado to herself and frowned at the young man, who was then led away by his bottle-blonde female companion.

Pete watched Gemma sit on one of the steps. He patted his back pockets and fished out a pack of cigarettes. 'You smoke?'

Gemma nodded. 'Sometimes.'

'Cool.' Pete continued to pat his pockets before running his hand inside his bomber jacket. 'Damn, no lighter.'

'That's not very slick,' Gemma teased, before handing Pete a lighter.

'Thanks,' Pete said, attempting to conceal his slight embarrassment. He sat beside Gemma, and she noticed him look her up and down before resting his eyes on her red fingernails, which were now clasped together on top of the black leggings wrapped around her surprisingly full thighs.

'Don't get any ideas.'

'What?' asked Pete. He lit his cigarette and was still looking at her thighs, and he was wondering how somebody so slim could have such womanly—

'Just because your friend was messing around with some girl out here doesn't mean that's what's going to happen between us.'

'What friend?' Pete noticed his voice had become involuntarily high-pitched as he attempted to gather his thoughts.

Gemma simply raised an eyebrow at him, and he suddenly found her even sexier.

Pete blew smoke out of his mouth and nostrils before passing the cigarette to Gemma. 'Oh that guy?' said Pete, pointing his thumb back towards the kitchen behind him. 'He's not my friend. I think he's in one of my classes—'

'I love this song!' Gemma jumped to her feet, dropping the cigarette, and as Pete began to realise Rod Stewart's *Passion* was flowing from the house, Gemma proceeded to sway to the music. She held out a hand, and although Pete never danced, that night was an exception. He didn't give a damn how out of time he was. He was dancing with this sexy out of towner whose lovely svelte body was enveloped in a leather biker jacket and black leggings. And he also didn't give a damn whether he was about to mess things up or not – there was no way he was going to pass up this opportunity to kiss her. And he did. Just like the cool dude who gets the girl in some of the movies he was obsessed with, he got Gemma. They missed the New Year's countdown and spent the chilly night kissing and talking about their mutual love of films.

Just like that night at the beginning of the year, Gemma and Pete were staring at the stars. This time they were sat in Pete's pride and joy, his 'Proud Mobile'. He called it this because, although it was five years old, Pete had used almost all of the money he had won from coming second in the 'Storytellers Of Tomorrow' short film competition. Gemma had seen the advert in the classifieds and brought it to Pete's attention.

Although she didn't understand what the hell the three minute film about a young man and a chair was supposed to represent, she was proud of her new boyfriend, and she told him this. So Pete decided to name his Hillman Avenger after her compliment.

'... Oooh ... yeah ...'

Gemma laughed as Pete attempted to sing along to Prince's lyrics. 'Thanks for tonight.'

After dinner the couple had gone to watch *On Golden Pond* at the cinema.

Pete switched off his headlights. 'No probs. I told you I'd take you out to celebrate all the good luck you've brought me.'

Gemma kissed Pete. 'So sweet.'

Pete grinned widely, 'And besides, I wanted you to see an example of my perfect sexy old woman!'

Gemma leaned away from Pete. 'Huh?'

Pete continued to grin.

'Jane Fonda's not that old!'

'No, no, no,' said Pete as he wagged a finger. 'I'm talking about Katharine Hepburn – now, if you look like that when you're her age I'll be a very happy man!'

Gemma laughed. 'First of all, yuck. And second, let's see if you're lucky enough to still know me then.'

Pete chuckled and feigned being shot in the chest before stealing a kiss from

Gemma. They took in the sight of each other – young, happy, and at the beginning of what they were sure was going to be one hell of an adventure.

'I love you,' said Gemma.

'I love you too,' said Pete. And then they kissed some more before making love in the back of Pete's Hillman Avenger.

FREDDIE, 1983

After almost a year, Freddie stopped asking questions. He was only ten years old but he could no longer be fooled. It soon became clear that each time his mother replied with 'Soon, he's just sorting out business,' she was lying. Grace was worn down by each untruth she told her son. Nine months ago, her husband, Frank, had returned home to Nigeria. Whenever the chubby Freddie would ask 'When is Daddy coming back?' she would fob him off with a piece of fiction. 'He's gone to Nigeria to build a house for us. It's taking longer than planned but he'll be back soon.' It was never Grace's intention to deceive her children. Part of her wanted to believe this was true – that her husband would be coming back – but she knew deep down that this wasn't the case.

On an already cold evening the central heating had broken down once again. Gathered in the tiny kitchen of their two-bedroom council flat – a flat so small that it would have quickly erased the fantasy Grace's family back in Nigeria had of England being the promised land – and wrapped in blankets, Grace sat Freddie and his skinny six-year-old sister, Chioma, down.

'Your father is not coming back.'

Freddie looked on, expressionless. It was then that he recalled the shouting and screaming that would take place between his parents.

While Freddie and Chioma were supposed to be asleep in the bedroom they shared, Grace and Frank would be arguing in the living room. Grace would scream something about Frank having been drinking in front of the television all day while she was out working. Frank would aggressively respond that he was trying and that this was no way to speak to a man. Freddie's mother would inform Frank that real men provided for their families and didn't gamble the rent on horses. Frank would mention the list of women that could confirm that he was a real man, and Freddie would hear some things breaking, before the front door would be opened and then slammed shut.

There was a particular night when Freddie's parent's played out their usual disputes. When he heard what sounded like glass being smashed and a chair being tipped over, Freddie quickly checked that Chioma was still asleep before running downstairs. By the time he got to the kitchen his father had already left the house. Freddie saw broken glass on the floor and his mother was sitting at the dining table crying. 'Be careful, don't come any closer!' she ordered Freddie as he approached her. 'There's glass everywhere, you'll hurt yourself!'

Ignoring her, Freddie rushed over and hugged his mother. She embraced him back, and as far as Freddie could remember, they cried all night.

When Grace had finally decided to come clean, she said, 'He's gone to Nigeria, and he's not coming back.' She fought back tears. 'He's left us.'

Chioma also started to cry.

Freddie looked at his mother and sister, their shoulders rising and falling as they sobbed. He was determined not to join in with the weeping. The man of the house by default, he put his short arms around them both.

'We'll be okay,' he said. 'I'll look after you.'

His mother stared up at him. As Freddie used his blanket to wipe her round, tear-stained face, he reflected on how his mother had never looked so childlike.

GEMMA AND PETE, WEDNESDAY 6 P.M.

Vivian patiently listened to Pete. She could see that there was something different about him this evening.

'Honestly, I'm so ashamed,' Pete said. 'He must have thought that I was some sort of deranged stalker.'

'Well,' Vivian began in a comforting tone, 'we can behave irrationally when we are desperate.'

Pete chuckled ruefully. 'Yeah.' He paused and stared at the wall behind Vivian, as if somewhere hidden within the cream paint was the answer to his next question. 'How could she lie like that?'

Vivian pursed her lips. 'Again, desperation leads to unreasonable behaviour.'

Pete shook his head. 'I'm not a violent person. I didn't even know that Kieran came here until Gemma mentioned it. I just felt like I had to be seen to be doing something after all the other times.'

Vivian continued to listen.

'I wanted to prove something to myself as much as anything else.' Pete let out a short and bitter laugh. 'I couldn't even manage that. I went for him in the car park and ended up on the floor.' Pete looked into Vivian's eyes and smiled. 'How embarrassing.'

Vivian observed Pete. Even though their conversation was of a sober nature, she had never heard him speak so freely.

'How could she lie?' Pete asked again.

'Gemma feels she's never got the reaction she wants from you. So she continues to push your buttons.'

Pete continued to look into Vivian's eyes.

'That's what I want to talk to the both of you about in this session.' Vivian glanced at her watch and frowned. 'Hopefully Gemma will be here soon and we can continue this conversation. But in the meantime I want you to tell me more about this job offer. I think it sounds like a good opportunity.' Vivian watched Pete as she waited for a response. He was looking significantly fresher. His brown hair was neatly combed and shinier than Vivian had ever seen it. And his face appeared less red and bloated.

Sitting opposite Vivian, minus Gemma, Pete continued to speak with more conviction than he had in previous sessions. 'It's just the stigma attached to directing soaps ...'

Vivian squinted at Pete, indicating that she wished to know more.

Pete gesticulated with his arms. 'They're not very ... how can I put it? Cutting edge. "Soap Land" is not exactly high art, is it?'

'Right ...' said Vivian.

There was a scratching sound as Pete rubbed the stubble on his face.

'Pete,' Vivian began, 'right now I think you should be commending the fact that you have been offered solid work. You love directing, and with this job you will have the opportunity to do what you love every day for the foreseeable future.'

'Yes, but how will it look?' Pete asked in a strained voice. 'This feels as if it's indicative of how far I've fallen. One step from Hollywood, all the way down to trashy TV.'

Vivian shook her head. 'I don't agree, Pete. I think this is a fantastic opportunity to put yourself back on the map and remind people what you can do.'

Pete clasped his hands in front of him. He slouched back into the sofa and, despite his tone, his body language appeared to demonstrate some sort of ease. 'But what about if a big gig comes up? I'll be unavailable if I take this job.'

Vivian smiled. 'Damned if you do, damned if you don't. The grass is always greener, eh?'

Vivian watched Pete smile again. The man sitting in front of her was an unburdened version of the man she had previously encountered. A man seemingly emancipated by the absence of his wife, and resuscitated by a new job opportunity.

Pete's smile faded slightly. 'I really thought it was movies for me next ...'

'You've had a difficult time recently work-wise.'

Pete looked at Vivian.

'Perhaps there's a part of you that has become used to the way it has made you feel – the suffering, the feeling sorry for yourself.'

Pete continued to stare at Vivian, listening intently.

'Maybe there is a perverse part of you that wants this to continue, so you can make excuses and keep telling yourself that an unfortunate sequence of events have prevented you from reaching your potential.'

Silence.

Vivian leaned forward. 'Maybe it will be a movie for you at some point. But right now, this is on the table. I don't think it'd be wise to discount what is there, for what might be around the corner.'

Pete bit his bottom lip as he nodded and held Vivian's gaze. The moment was interrupted by a knock on the door. Before waiting for an answer, Gemma burst into the room.

'Sorry I'm late—'

'What was it this time?' Pete asked through gritted teeth. 'Were you involved in an imaginary group shag with Kieran Ledley and his teammates? Or were you in the real world this time with people who are actually in your league?'

Vivian attempted to stop Pete's questioning from turning into a rant, 'Okay, Pete —'

'Did Steve's car break down?' Pete continued, 'Did you guys stop off for a quick one before he dropped you here—'

Gemma turned to her husband. 'Fuck you—'

'Or were you with Tim today?' Pete added.

Vivian stood up. 'Please, can we all just take a step back?'

Silence fell over the room. Gemma walked over to the sofa and sat on it, trying to keep as much distance between herself and Pete as possible. Vivian watched as Pete scanned his wife, as if he was looking for telltale signs of another man. Gemma ignored his scrutiny, opting to stare ahead at the wall behind Vivian.

Sitting back down, Vivian said, 'Gemma, it's important that you and Pete attend these sessions together.'

Gemma cleared her throat and attempted to adopt a dignified tone. 'Yes Vivian, again, I apologise.'

'Okay, Gemma,' Vivian replied as she picked up her file. 'I really would appreciate a bit more effort as it's the second time this has happened now.'

Gemma breathed in, looking irked. She cleared her throat once more, adjusted her rumpled white blouse and took a quick glance at Pete before muttering, 'Oh God.'

Vivian flicked through her file. 'So Gemma—'

'How much time has he spent going on about this new job offer of his?' Gemma looked at her watch and turned to Pete. 'Come on, how much have you been hamming up your new so-called triumph?'

'When did I ever call it a triumph?' Pete replied, throwing an incredulous look towards Vivian. He turned back to Gemma. 'You patronising, heartless bitch.'

Stung by his words, Gemma looked at Vivian. 'Have you noticed the way he has been speaking to me lately?' Her bottom lip began to tremble. 'I'm sure you have. He's lost all respect for me. And now this job comes along and you cast me aside even further.'

Pete put his face in his hands. 'You are unbelievable.'

Vivian observed the couple. She took in Gemma, who appeared to be fighting back tears, and she looked at Pete, who put his hands down, revealing his reddening face, his relaxed body language now a thing of the recent past.

'Respect?' Pete asked, still incredulous. 'You have the nerve to talk to me about respect?'

'Gemma?' Vivian said, 'do you not think that this is good news for your husband?'

Vivian watched Gemma rifle through her handbag. Assuming she was looking for a handkerchief, Vivian grabbed a box of tissues from the desk behind her and handed them over.

'Thank you,' Gemma said, as she wiped her tears.

'Gemma, do you want your husband's career to pick up again, or not?'

Gemma blew her nose and looked up at Vivian. 'I guess I'll just have to prepare myself to get left behind like the last time he was working.'

DAILY REFLECTION

Saturday, 22nd October, 2011

FOOTBALL STAR'S FATHER DIES IN HORROR CAR

CRASH

Nigel Ledley, father of Authenton FC striker, Kieran Ledley, died in a car crash in the early hours of this morning. He was airlifted to Midsten Hospital but was pronounced dead on arrival.

The collision occurred on the A12, between Romford in Essex and the M25, which is a notorious accident hotspot. Two other cars were involved in the pile-up. Husband and wife Christopher and Bridget Lancaster, both aged 38, were also pronounced dead at the scene. Another man who has not yet been named is said to be in a critical but stable condition.

Nigel Ledley is thought to have been on his way to watch his son's away match at Daggerton Rovers. The 58-year-old adopted Kieran, whose biological parents are of British and Caribbean descent, when he was 5 years old.

A family friend said, 'This tragic event has devastated the whole family, and will hit Kieran particularly hard. Despite all his success, Kieran had remained close to his father.'

Kieran's adoptive mother, Anna Ledley, is said to be inconsolable. Her oldest son, Kieran's stepbrother, Callum Ledley, is currently serving a two-year jail sentence for armed robbery.

Kieran's representatives could not be reached but a club spokesman said, 'This is a truly difficult time for Mr Ledley. Our thoughts are with him and his family.'

When asked whether Kieran will be playing in this afternoon's game, the spokesman declined to comment.

PETE / FREDDIE

'Sorry, mate,' Freddie said as the door hit him. The exiting punter simply nodded. Freddie had been standing outside the pub for almost five minutes. Conscious of the fact that he hadn't attended his local since his attack, Freddie was determined to show his face. Yes, he was hardly a regular, and yes he was wearing a faded blue baseball cap, but he wanted to demonstrate that he wasn't a paranoid MP living in exile. Freddie pulled the semi-disguise a little further down his face and walked in.

The place was loud and busy, and the crowd was a mix of Woundham regulars and people enjoying after-work drinks. Freddie looked up at the big screen and could see that there was a football match being played. He approached the shiny wooden bar, all the while looking left and right as he squeezed past the evening drinkers, wondering if anybody recognised him.

'Gin and Tonic, please,' Freddie politely ordered from the skinny young barman.

'What?' the barman called over the noise.

Freddie raised his voice, 'G and T, please.'

The barman nodded and Freddie leaned against the bar attempting to relax and take in the game.

'Another chance goes begging. Kieran Ledley really isn't himself today. It's very brave of him to be playing after the tragic loss of his father less than a week ago. But the manager must surely be thinking it's time to make a substitution ...'

As Freddie collected his drink he suddenly felt as if he was being watched. He looked over to his right and further along the bar he could see a man staring at him. Taking a sip of his drink and adjusting his cap again, Freddie did his best to remain calm. He continued to watch the football match, and when from the corner of his eye he could see the man approaching him through the crowd, Freddie did what he could to recall his 'Unflappable Politician Stance'.

'Freddie Abani?'

Freddie glanced up from under his cap.

'I thought it was you.'

Freddie took in the sight of the large, tall white man in his forties.

'I just want to say that I admire you a lot.' The man smiled, put his pint on the bar and held out a hand. 'Pete Newman.'

Freddie looked around the lively pub. Though he was somewhat relieved, he hoped that this wasn't going to be the catalyst for unwanted attention. He shook Pete's hand tentatively.

'Sorry, you probably get this all the time,' Pete said with a smile.

Freddie frowned and let out a little laugh. 'No. Not lately anyway.'

Pete took a sip of his beer. 'It really was a surreal summer. Honestly, when I was watching the riots on TV I couldn't believe that this was happening in England, literally on our doorstep … amazing.'

Freddie cleared his throat. 'Well, yes it's been—'

Just then, Freddie was interrupted by a collective groan from the revellers.

'Fuck's sake! Get that flipping prima donna off!' shouted a stocky man from the corner of the bar.

Pete pointed towards the large screen, where Kieran Ledley could be seen looking towards the heavens and shaking his head. He smiled and turned to Freddie. 'My wife claimed she was having an affair with that guy.'

Freddie frowned 'What?'

Pete chuckled to himself. 'She's crazy.'

Freddie sipped from his glass and blinked in confusion.

'You into football, then?' Pete asked.

'Not really,' Freddie confessed in between sips. 'I mean, I used to follow it a bit but, you know …'

Pete nodded. 'The game has lost its soul if you ask me. But still, nothing like a bit of Champions League, eh?'

Freddie adjusted his cap. 'Yeah, definitely.'

Pete smiled. 'You did know this was a Champions League match, right?'

Freddie cleared his throat again. 'Yes, of course.'

Pete laughed. 'Course you did!' He pointed at Freddie's glass. 'Fancy another?'

'I'm fine, actually. I have an early start—'

'Go on,' said Pete. 'I'm sure you've had a busy day. Let your hair down.'

Before Freddie could protest, Pete was already in the middle of getting the barman's attention.

'And Ledley sends the free kick high and wide.'

'What a pile of shit!' The insult once again came from the stocky man at the corner of the bar. When he saw Freddie looking at him, he took a large gulp of beer before saying, 'What the fuck are you staring at?'

Freddie paused before sighing. He held up both hands. 'Nothing.'

'That's what I thought.' And with that the stocky man fixed his gaze back on the big screen.

Pete returned with a beer and another G and T for Freddie.

'Thanks,' Freddie said as he received the drink.

Pete raised his glass. 'No problem.' He took a sip. 'I'm a film-maker by the way.'

'Oh right,' Freddie said without taking his eyes off the screen.

Pete rubbed his jaw. 'Yeah, I direct a TV show at the moment but my background is in documentaries.'

Freddie adjusted his cap.

'I don't know if you're into any of that stuff,' Pete continued, 'but I've been toying with the idea of making a film about the riots.'

Freddie turned to him. He wasn't sure how he felt about the information he was receiving. 'Really?'

'Yeah,' Pete replied. 'I know there've been a few out already but they seemed a little rushed, and biased if you ask me. People seem to want to stay away from the Devon Constance killing, but I think it's wrong to avoid a very important part of the story.'

Freddie's interest was piqued, but still aware of the somewhat public nature of their conversation, he simply nodded and drank.

'I don't know if you have a PA, or someone who takes care of your media work but I'd love to—

'Finally!' The stocky man's voice could be heard again.

'A dejected-looking Kieran Ledley is going off. I think sympathetic is the best way to describe the applause as he approaches the touchline. And it appears to be coming from both sets of fans.'

'Fucking overpaid monkey!'

Pete placed his beer on the bar. 'Hey, there's no need for that.'

Freddie held an arm out in front of Pete. 'It's not worth it. Just leave it.'

'No, hang on,' said Pete, 'he's being out of order.'

'And what the fuck are you going to do about it?' The stocky man stumbled up from his stool and also fell into a group of ladies as he attempted to make his way over.

'Watch out!' shouted one of the ladies, who followed this up with a push. The stocky man then fell back into another man, causing him to spill his drink all over his suit.

'Oh for goodness sake!' The man looked down at his drenched shirt and blazer before grabbing the stocky man.

Freddie took in the ensuing altercation before turning to Pete. 'Look, I think I'm going to go home. Thanks for the drink.'

As Freddie battled his way through the agitated crowd, Pete called after him, 'Hang on, how can I get in touch with you?'

Freddie heard him but simply pulled his cap down some more and breathed a sigh of relief when he reached the exit.

VIVIAN / GEMMA

Vivian stepped into her car and sat behind the wheel. She switched on her headlights, brightening up the dark car park. As she was about to turn the key in the ignition she was startled by a thump at her window.

'Vivian!'

Her heart skipped a beat as a face appeared. It was Gemma.

'Gemma?' Vivian peered through the glass. 'Is that you?'

'Yes. Vivian, I need to talk to you.'

Vivian pressed a button and the window began to lower. She looked at Gemma's puffy eyes. 'Gemma? What is it?'

'It's Pete ... I think he's having an affair.'

Vivian sighed and attempted to hide her exasperation. 'I've finished work for the day, Gemma. It's quite late. I'm on my way—'

'I think he's been sleeping with that slut, Amanda Jenkins.' Gemma could read Vivian's confused expression. 'You know? The actress. She plays Kitty, the girl who works behind the bar on his show.'

Vivian sighed again. 'Right … I'm not familiar—'

'You don't watch it?' Gemma interrupted. 'I don't blame you, it's a load of rubbish.'

'Gemma, I really must get home. I can't discuss you and Pete outside of our sessions. You both have to be present—'

Vivian was once again cut short, but this time it was by Gemma's tears. 'How dare he?!' Gemma blubbed. 'How can he do this to me? It's revenge. The bastard!' she began to wail.

'Gemma, please.' Vivian looked around the car park. 'Please, try and calm down …' Vivian looked on as Gemma walked round to the passenger side of the car and let herself in. She sat down next to Vivian.

'How did he even get her?' Gemma asked, through tears and mucus. 'She's so young, and pretty.' She reached into her handbag and brought out her phone. 'Look,' she started to wave the phone in front of Vivian. 'This is a picture of the bitch.'

'Gemma, stop it. There's no need for that.'

'Just look!' Gemma shouted, wielding the phone.

'Stop it.' Vivian said as calmly as she could. She placed her hands on the steering wheel, and both women sat in silence for a few moments.

Vivian leaned over and brought out a pack of tissues from the glove compartment. She handed them to Gemma.

'He's changed,' Gemma sniffed. She began to wipe her face. 'Ever since the day he grabbed me in your office.' She looked at Vivian, who remained silent.

'It's as if he was awoken that day. Like something snapped inside of him.'

Vivian considered her patient. Gemma was getting thinner by the day and the bones in her shoulders jutted out when she blew her nose.

But for Gemma's intermittent sniffing, both woman now sat in silence as a cool breeze drifted in through the window. Gemma lay back on the passenger seat and listened to the distant sound of traffic.

After some time, Vivian decided to say, 'That story you made up about you and Kieran—'

Gemma sat up. 'I just wanted my husband to look at me—'

'That's not the way, Gemma.' Vivian interjected. 'I don't appreciate you using another patient of mine in your juvenile and dishonest games—'

'I know,' Gemma replied sheepishly.

'I hope so,' Vivian went on. 'My patients have enough on their plates without having to be dragged into your issues.'

Gemma simply nodded and sucked in her cheeks, making it look like her cheekbones were about to pierce through her skin.

She put her hand on the door handle and was about to open it when she said, 'Now he's got this new job, he's coming home late, dressing well, walking around with a new swagger.' Gemma stared out at the car park, tracing the beams of light from Vivian's vehicle to the number plate of a car in front. 'He's buzzing again. The way he used to be when he'd finished film school and we'd just met.'

Tired, Vivian looked at Gemma's delicate silhouette.

'It's as if ...' Gemma searched for the end of her sentence. She turned to Vivian. 'It's as if he doesn't need me anymore.'

KIERAN AND CALLUM, 2011

Anna Ledley stood weeping next to her handcuffed son. Two prison officers flanked Callum. He had been granted temporary release for the funeral of his father. Nigel Ledley's coffin lay in the centre of the large gathering of relatives. There was a hum of crying as the priest read from the bible, '... let us commend Nigel's body to the mercy of God ...'

Callum was serving the final three months of his fifth prison sentence as an adult. This time it was for possession of a deadly weapon and vehicular theft. He looked at the heaving shoulders of his relatives, some he didn't recognise, and most of whom he hadn't seen since he was a child. He spotted Fat Uncle Charlie with his arm around a young boy.

He remembered how his uncle used to bring sweets round for him and Kieran when they were kids. He saw a now grown-up female cousin, dabbing her tears with a handkerchief.

Callum looked up at the grey sky casting a dull gloom over the graveyard. He felt the cold wind slide over his bony pale face and took a deep breath. The setting couldn't be more depressing but there was nothing like the smell of freedom, albeit temporary.

Autumn leaves drifted past as Callum scanned the relatives gathered around the coffin once more. His gaze rested on a familiar aunty who, once their eyes met, returned a look of disdain, before looking away. Callum thought about how none of the family present had ever visited him in jail. He started to fill with anger as he contemplated the rejection from his so-called loved ones.

He turned to the one person who he was sure still loved him – his mother. He smiled at her. Her gaunt face was wet with tears, and she stared at her son with her bloodshot eyes before taking a quick glance at the expressionless prison officers.

A black four-by-four with tinted windows pulled up in the distance. The driver stepped out and opened the door at the back. Callum looked on as an overweight man hopped out of the vehicle. He wasn't one hundred per cent sure but he was quite certain that this was Nathan Rougel, his brother's agent. He remembered him from when they were children. He remembered the day that a strange fat man had approached Kieran at the park.

That day, Callum had run over to his younger brother and thrown a protective arm around him. 'We don't talk to strangers,' he had said, backing himself and Kieran away.

'Of course,' the fat man had replied, before reaching into the inside pocket of his blazer. 'I'm a football agent.'

Callum remembered how the man had brought out a business card, *just like they did in the movies.*

'I think your friend here has talent.'

'He's not my friend, he's my brother,' Callum had replied with attitude.

'Really?' the fat man had asked, looking at the two boys, one white, and one mixed race.

'Yeah.'

'In that case, tell your parents to give me a call.' He handed his card over, turned to Kieran, and held out his hand. 'Cool, man.'

Kieran had looked at Callum before shaking the stranger's hand.

Back in the present, Callum saw the man mouth something to whoever was in the vehicle. Then out stepped Kieran Ledley, wearing dark shades and dressed in a black suit. This was the first time Callum had seen his stepbrother in the flesh for nine years. As he watched him approach, he then noticed that there was a tall, powerfully built white man, who was also wearing shades, following Kieran and Nathan.

The priest continued to lead the service in the background as Kieran hugged his mother. The brothers stood face to face. Callum looked at Kieran, his younger brother's expression hidden behind his dark shades.

Pursing his lips, and without saying a word, Kieran hugged Callum.

Telling himself that he would have returned the embrace had his hands not been cuffed in front of him, Callum now felt his mother join in. The three of them were reunited.

'Ashes to ashes,' the priest called out as he threw dirt on the casket with a small spade. 'Dust to dust.'

Callum looked on as the priest passed the spade to Fat Uncle Charlie. After wiping his eyes and sprinkling dirt on the coffin, Fat Uncle Charlie passed the spade to Kieran. The wind caused the dirt to scatter slightly as Kieran tipped the spade down towards the coffin. He turned to Callum and looked down at his handcuffed wrists. 'Have some respect,' he said, looking at the prison officers standing either side of his stepbrother.

The officers looked at each other.

'It's our father's funeral for God's sake,' Kieran said, removing his shades.

There was a pause before one of the officers said to the other, 'It's Kieran effin' Ledley.' The star-struck officer fished a bunch of keys out of his pocket and removed Callum's handcuffs.

Anna, and the rest of the family gathered, looked on as Callum adjusted his wrists and took the spade from Kieran.

As the burial came to a close, Kieran stared at Callum. He didn't know what to say. He was embarrassed, and the more he thought about it, he was intimidated. 'How are you?' he managed to ask.

'I've been better,' Callum replied.

Kieran looked at his stepbrother staring at him. It was a deep and penetrating gaze, as if he was scanning him internally.

'But I've been worse,' Callum continued before flashing a brief smile, which revealed his browning teeth.

Callum's prison officers stood a few yards away by a tree. By another tree stood Nathan Rougel and Kieran's bodyguard. They looked over at their respective subjects, supervising them for reasons that couldn't be more different.

'I don't think your babysitters want you to be talking to me,' Callum said, taking in Nathan and the powerfully built man beside him.

Kieran shook his head. 'I'm sorry about everything.'

There was a moment of silence before Callum pointed at Nathan. 'Isn't that the guy from the park?'

'Yeah,' Kieran replied. 'You remember?'

The pause, and the stare. 'Memories are all I have,' said Callum.

Kieran followed Callum's fixed look to his mother, surrounded by family, a sea of sombre-looking faces, dressed in black.

'So what happened?' Callum asked Kieran. 'They don't allow football players to pick up a pen these days?'

'What do you mean?' Kieran replied.

Callum frowned bitterly. 'You never replied to any of my letters.'

Before Kieran could reply, a flash came from the direction of another tree.

'Hey!' Kieran's bodyguard shouted. He ran towards the direction of the bright light and tackled a much smaller man who was holding a black object.

'Get the fuck off me!' The man groaned, gasping for air as Kieran's bodyguard pinned him to the ground and pressed his knee into his back.

'I know your face now,' the bodyguard said as he removed the memory card from the man's camera. 'Don't let me see you again.'

'Fuck off!' The man groaned again. 'I'm just doing my job.'

'And I'm doing mine,' Kieran's bodyguard said as Nathan and the prison guards came over.

The mourning was briefly distracted by the disturbance.

Callum looked at Kieran's bodyguard roughly drag the photographer up from the ground. 'Looks like it was you who brought the trouble today,' he said in what Kieran perceived to be an ironic tone.

'Shit, damn press,' Kieran sighed as he watched the photographer trudge off.

GEMMA AND PETE

From her vantage point Gemma could make out the figure of her husband. He was walking alongside a petite, brown-haired young woman. Gemma was certain this was Amanda Jenkins. She was also certain that she could see her husband look from side to side, before leaning in for a quick kiss from Amanda.

Gemma tried to control her breathing as she played the conversation she imagined Pete was having with Amanda in her head. The petite woman went into a building and Gemma kept her eyes on Pete as he headed towards his car. She ducked, making sure she was out of her husband's eyeline as he entered his vehicle and started the engine. As he pulled away into the darkness, Gemma put her car into gear and followed him. They drove for a short while and Gemma began to recognise the route.

'Fucking prick,' she muttered to herself, 'he's going home.' She inhaled deeply. 'To our fucking home.'

Gemma hung back as Pete pulled into the driveway of their house. Parked around the corner, she craned her neck and watched Pete disappear inside.

Pete stretched as he entered the narrow hallway. He looked towards the stairs and peered into the small living room. He frowned, nonchalantly noting that his wife wasn't home. He walked into the kitchen and flicked the light on, removing his new black leather jacket and placing it on the back of one of the dining chairs.

Puffing his cheeks, he walked over to the counter and uncorked a bottle of red wine.

He grabbed a glass and sat at his dining table, reflecting on what a good day it had been. As he filled his glass he smiled. He was starting to feel something that resembled happiness, an emotion that had evaporated from his life a long time ago. A feeling that he couldn't imagine experiencing again. He was busy once more, working with creatives. He felt important, like he mattered.

He was enjoying himself and he was getting on very well with his colleagues, especially Amanda. Pete thought about how glad he was that he had accepted the job. As he rubbed his face and took a large sip of wine he remembered his former therapist's good advice. He and Gemma had stopped seeing Vivian. After Gemma continued to turn up late, and sometimes not turn up at all, Pete decided that it was a waste of money.

'Oh, so now you're earning a bit of cash that's all you care about?!' Gemma had spewed at Pete when he suggested they stopped attending marriage counselling. 'It's me that has kept us afloat all this time. While you've been spending all day in front of your laptop for "research". While you've been doing fuck all. You remember that!'

Pete shook his head as he continued to drink. It wasn't just the money. It was the fact that he thought maybe now he was working all their problems would be solved. At his lowest points he would convince himself that once he was back on his feet he would be able to address their marriage. And he'd now come to the conclusion that that's what he wanted. He wanted his wife back. He wanted to be able to look after her like he had promised when they met. Pete smiled as he recalled how quickly they'd fallen in love.

At one stage their trips around the world had felt like a tour of excitement, rushes, and thrills. He wanted that back. Pete looked around his kitchen and suddenly began to wonder where his wife was at this moment? Was she with Steve, or Tim? Or someone else?

He wondered if he was a fool to think their marriage could be salvaged at all, that they could return to the glory days of the eighties when they were young lovers. The nineties, when Pete's ambitions became even more audacious and attractive to Gemma, before the first cracks started to appear three years ago.

Pete downed the rest of his glass and began to refill it. As he started to question whether he preferred when they were boyfriend and girlfriend, then eventually 'partners', to being married – it was so grown-up, and he liked the idea of being an artist that didn't have to grow up – he heard the key turn in the front door.

'Gem?' he called.

Gemma walked into the kitchen and looked at him sitting at the table. She looked at his jacket on the back of the chair. 'Nice jacket. A bit young for you though, don't you think?'

'Gemma,' Pete replied in between sips, 'don't start. Not tonight, okay?' He watched her walk over to a cabinet and take out a glass. As she headed towards him at the table, he held out the bottle. 'Do you want me to fill you up?'

'I can do it myself.' Gemma aggressively snatched it from him and began to fill her glass. She took a large gulp and slowly walked over to the kitchen doorway.

Pete watched her. To him, she looked as if she had been crying, but he couldn't be sure because it was a look that she had worn for as long as he could remember. 'Why don't you join me, Gem? Sit down.'

Gemma remained silent, instead slowly sipping and training her eyes on her husband.

Pete began to feel uncomfortable. 'Fine, if you're going to be like that I'm going to bed.'

'How was work today?' Gemma asked as her husband stood up.

'Fine,' he replied, grabbing his jacket.

'You get all the scenes done?'

Pete eyed Gemma with suspicion. 'Erm … Yeah. We did.'

'Good,' Gemma replied. 'That's good.'

'Don't take the piss out of me, Gemma. I don't appreciate it.'

'What's your problem?' Gemma asked. 'Is it a crime for me to ask my husband how his day was?'

Pete looked down towards the table. He sighed and was about to speak when Gemma said, 'What time did you get in this evening?'

Pete shrugged. 'Quite a while ago.'

'What time?' Gemma asked again.

'I'm really not in the mood for this—'

Gemma marched over to the table. 'Don't fucking lie to me!'

'Lie to you about what?!' Pete replied, matching his wife's volume. 'Why are you shouting?'

'Because you are fucking lying to me!'

'What are you talking about?!' Pete asked.

Gemma slammed her glass down on the wooden table that separated them.

The glass shattered and its contents spilled onto the table and down onto the kitchen tiles. 'You didn't get home a while ago, you only just got home. I followed you from the studio.'

'You did what?' Pete asked, taken aback.

'I followed you from the studio, you fucking prick,' Gemma hissed. 'And I saw you with that whore. I know you took her back to her apartment.'

Pete held his arms up. 'We went for a drink. There were a few script changes that she was unsure about so we—'

'Spare me the arty crap! You're fucking her, aren't you?'

Pete smiled ruefully. 'This is ridiculous. I'm going to walk away and give you some time to calm down.'

Gemma grabbed Pete as he attempted to walk past her. 'Don't you walk away from me, you bastard.' She got hold of the front of his shirt as he turned towards her. 'I know you're fucking her to get your own back on me, you sick bastard!' Gemma screamed as she ripped his shirt.

Pete pushed her off and held her arms by her side. He shook her forcefully. 'Don't put your guilt on me. I'm not fucking anyone. Don't fucking do it!' Saliva framed both of their mouths as they stared at each other, panting. 'I'm going to bed.'

Pete turned his back on Gemma and went to walk away. As he did so, Gemma grabbed the bottle from the table and screamed as she smashed it over her husband's head. The bottle exploded as it connected with the back of Pete's skull and the remaining wine sprayed everywhere. Pete dropped to the ground, cracking his forehead on the thick counter along the way.

Gemma looked at the heap on the kitchen floor. Her husband was lying face down, the blood pouring from his head, travelling along the gaps of the dark-brown tiles. She held up her trembling, bleeding hand. Rooted to the spot, she attempted to bring her breathing under control. Lightheaded, Gemma took unsteady steps towards the doorway. She climbed up the stairs and tripped as she made her way to the bedroom.

Her hands continued to quiver as she ripped the drawers out of the cabinets. She finally found the bottle of pills she was looking for. She grabbed them and headed back down the stairs and into the kitchen. Gemma stepped over Pete's body and went over to the counter where she picked up another bottle of red wine and uncorked it with her bloodied hand. She popped open the bottle of pills and emptied every single one into her mouth. She walked back over to her sprawled out husband and sat next to him on the ground. Queasy, Gemma fished her phone out of her pocket and stared at it before dialling 999.

'Nine, nine, nine emergency. Which service please?' the controller spoke through the phone.

'Ambulance please,' Gemma replied as she felt her eyelids become heavy. 'There's been an accident.' Gemma began to pour the bottle of wine down her throat. The room slowly began to spin as she lay down beside her husband. Her mobile fell from her hand, and Gemma blacked out.

'Hello? Madam? Madam? Are you still there?'

FREDDIE 2011

Freddie sat in the back of the black taxi on his way to yet another meeting with the head of the IPCC. He pulled out his vibrating phone from the breast pocket of his grey blazer. The screen read *MUM*. He quickly glanced at his watch. Knowing that he was already running behind schedule, he cancelled the call.

Freddie didn't speak to his mother often enough, and when they did talk, it was usually a long conversation, with a significant amount of it spent listening to Grace lambasting him for not calling her more frequently. Although it had been his New Year's resolution to address this, now was not the time. Freddie briefly looked out the window as the taxi stuttered its way through congested Holborn. The sun was shy and hiding behind the clouds. When he was about to return the phone to his pocket, it vibrated again.

He looked at the screen and once more *MUM was* illuminated on the display.

He frowned; normally she would accidentally leave him a voicemail, which would consist of her saying *'Hello? Hello? Freddie?'* before ending with a tut.

Freddie answered the call. 'Mum,' he said, holding the phone to his ear, 'I'm on my way to a meeting. I promise I'll call you back as soon as I'm out.'

'He's gone,' replied his mother's weak voice.

Freddie shut his eyes. He knew immediately that his mother was talking about his father.

'Are you there?' Grace asked him.

Freddie cleared his throat and blinked. 'Yes, mum, I'm here. How did he go?'

'They found him in his sleep, they-they …' Freddie's mother stammered, *'they think he may have drowned in his own vomit.'*

Freddie adjusted his glasses. 'Are you okay, Mum?'

'Yes,' she replied.

'Have you spoken to Chioma?'

'Yes,' Grace sniffed, *'she's on her way over.'*

'Okay. I'll be there after my meeting.'

'Okay,' Grace replied, in an appreciative tone.

'I love you, Mum.'

'I love you, too.'

Freddie listened to his mother hang up. Sadly twirling his mobile phone in his hand, he pictured an old version of his father. He saw a pathetic image of him lying in bed covered in vomit, in the small room of a house in a Nigerian village.

DAILY REFLECTION

Tuesday, 1st November, 2011

AWARD-WINNING DIRECTOR AND WIFE FOUND DEAD

AT HOME

British film-maker Pete Newman, 42, and his wife Gemma Newman, 39, were found dead at the home they shared in Welwynshire, Greater London, last night.

At 10.03 p.m., paramedics arrived on the scene fourteen minutes after receiving the emergency call from Mrs Newman. The police arrived at the house not long after.

A Welwynshire police spokesman told how they were made aware of the distress call by the operator. 'We had the emergency call sent over to us and we acted as soon as possible. Mrs Newman had simply told the operator that there had been an accident, before the line went dead. We are treating this as a murder inquiry but at the moment we do not believe anybody else is involved.'

When asked if he thought this was a murder–suicide, the spokesman replied, 'It would seem so, yes.'

Newman won acclaim for his work on the 2008 film *The Smell of Danger*. After disappearing from the scene, he returned to directing earlier this year, working on the popular soap *Saint Narcissists*. The controller of drama for

UKtelevisual said, 'This is truly a shock. We are all devastated by this horrific news. It really is hard to comprehend. The show's producers, the actors and I have agreed that it is only right we suspend filming until further notice.'

A post-mortem is due to be carried out this afternoon.

Pete and Gemma are thought to have been married for almost ten years, and moved into the semi-detached property three to four years ago. A neighbour – who did not wish to be named – said, 'This is a fairly quiet area. Couples tend to come here to settle down or to start a family. The fact that raised voices could often be heard coming from their [Mr and Mrs Newman's] house is something the residents often gossiped about amongst themselves.'

Another neighbour, Joanne Sonti, 28, said, 'There was a lot of shouting last night. I could hear her [Gemma's] voice mainly. I wasn't too alarmed by this, she was always shouting, and there have been times when I've seen them arguing in the street. They seemed alright, but they didn't really talk to the other neighbours much. I just took it that they were quite private, him working on TV and that. And anyway, those media types can be quite dramatic, innit?'

Mr Newman's agent couldn't be reached for comment.

The director and his wife are not thought to have had any children.

FREDDIE, THURSDAY 1 P.M.

Freddie walked into Vivian's office. 'Before you ask, yes, I'm ready to talk about my father.'

Vivian watched him calmly walk over to the sofa.

He removed his blazer and sat down. 'He died earlier this week.'

Vivian clasped her hands and looked down briefly before asking, 'How do you feel about that?'

Freddie stared at the cream wall behind her.

After a long pause, he said, 'Angry that I'll never be able to tell him how we all felt about him deserting us. Sad that I'll never be able to let him know that I think he's a piece of shit …' Freddie put his head in his hands and took a deep breath. He exhaled slowly before slightly chuckling to himself. 'I guess my to-do list just got a little lighter.'

Vivian smiled and nodded sympathetically.

'I've been spending a lot of time with my mum and sister. I'm so proud of us. The way we've turned out.'

Vivian smiled.

'I remember all the times I had to take Chioma to school. We always had to run for the number forty-nine bus,' Freddie squinted as he brought up the image, 'and it always seemed to be winter.' He laughed quietly.

Vivian poured him a glass of water.

Freddie nodded appreciatively and continued. 'When we got home I'd have to warm up our food. Without fail it was chicken and mushroom pie, and it only needed twenty minutes in the oven but I'd always burn it!'

'That's men for you.' Vivian smiled again. 'Keep them away from the kitchen, I say.'

'That's sexist!' Freddie laughed.

'Yes, it's a sexist truth!' Vivian replied. They both laughed, then a silence fell over the room.

Freddie tilted his head to the side. 'I only really remember seeing my mum in the mornings. She was always working.

She couldn't even afford to take time off for parents' evenings. I don't know how she could have ever had time for any friends. She sacrificed everything for us.'

Vivian leaned forward. 'Maybe she was so focused on keeping a roof over your heads that she didn't see it as a sacrifice.'

Freddie bit his bottom lip. 'Hmm …' He shook his head. 'I can't imagine what it must be like to only be able to send your babies off to school with a kiss, then head off to work – which would consist of scrubbing floors all day – only to return to them fast asleep. How … lonely.'

'It must have been incredibly difficult,' Vivian said, 'but I'm sure there must have been a part of your mother that was simply relieved whenever she came home to find you guys safe, whether you were asleep or not.' Vivian watched Freddie nodding before his expression slowly morphed into anger.

'The last time I saw my father he was lying on the living room sofa. There was saliva around his mouth and he had a bottle of whisky on his chest. I remember being disgusted by the smell.' Freddie paused. 'He's being buried in his village. We're not going to the funeral.'

'That's your right,' Vivian replied.

'We don't have any respects to pay,' Freddie said in a stoical tone.

'I understand,' said Vivian, 'and if you ever change your mind about that in the future, that's fine too. Remember, Freddie, you don't have anything to prove.'

DAILY REFLECTION
Friday, 4th November, 2011

THE SUPERSTAR AND THE CRIMINAL

This is the moment Premier League superstar Kieran Ledley and his brother Callum, 27, were reunited. Callum Ledley, who is serving the final months of a jail sentence for armed robbery, was granted special leave for the day to attend his father's funeral.

Nigel Ledley was killed in a horrific smash, which involved two other vehicles, on the A12 between Romford in Essex and the M25, two weeks ago.

Callum's prison officers can be seen in the background. The stepbrothers are said to have been estranged for almost a decade.

Kieran Ledley, the world's most expensive football player, with reported earnings of over £200,000 a week, couldn't have a more contrasting life to that of his adopted brother.

Callum has been in and out of prison since his mid-teens. His crimes include drug possession with intent to supply and aggravated assault.

Kieran Ledley is due to return to action for the first time since bravely taking to the pitch in Authenton's Champions League defeat against Spain's Matador Gomera. The winger is expected to start in this weekend's away clash at Shrewten Athletic.

VIVIAN

After her breakthrough with Freddie, Vivian realised it was time for a progression of her own. She had long considered David as her ex-husband, but they were still married.

Vivian sat behind her steering wheel. She reached over to the glove compartment of her car and pulled out a brown envelope. She took a deep breath and looked around the car park. 'Come on,' Vivian quietly mumbled to herself before stepping out of her car.

Vivian joined the line of people entering the imposing building. She pulled her grey coat tightly around her as the wind stroked her face and body.

The line was made up of mostly women, but there were also a few men and small children.

'Arms out.'

On entering the building Vivian did as instructed and the female warden searched her. Even though this wasn't the first time that Vivian had visited this prison, it was something she knew she could never get used to. She could feel her heartbeat speed up as the warden finished patting her down.

'Okay, move on, please.'

Vivian approached a counter.

'Identification, please,' the lady requested from behind the glass screen.

Vivian handed over her driver's licence and passport.

After looking them over, the woman said, 'Visiting order?'

Vivian continued to look through the glass at the woman, observing the casual manner with which she was going about her job. The woman's hair was scraped back into a short ponytail, and she was expressionless.

'Visiting order, madam?'

'Oh yes,' Vivian replied, snapping out of her momentary inattentiveness. She handed the document over.

The lady behind the glass partition scanned the documents before looking up at Vivian with a hint of a smile. 'Okay.' She slid Vivian's items back under the partition. 'Go through.' She then pressed a buzzer and Vivian was escorted by a thickset male prison officer to the visitors' room.

Vivian looked around the busy room. She saw a man hugging a woman.

She saw another man give a little girl a kiss. She looked at these people and wondered what each individual story was. Vivian wondered if any of the other men in the room where serving time for domestic violence. She also wondered how some of the reunited families could look so happy.

The thickset prison officer stepped to the side when he and Vivian arrived at a table.

'Hi.'

Vivian looked at the man whom the greeting belonged to. Her husband had put on weight in the last five months since she had seen him. His face was fuller, and though he had grown his beard and hair, both were neat. Vivian cast her eyes over his slightly dry, sand-coloured face. 'Hello David.'

They sat in silence for a moment and Vivian glanced around the room once more. She suddenly felt awkward as she saw a man and woman holding hands across a table.

'How's work?' David asked.

'Busy,' Vivian replied.

'That's good,' said David. 'I know you like to keep busy.'

Vivian attempted a smile. 'How are you?'

David held his wife's gaze for the first time since she sat down. He shrugged, and there was a brief pause before he said, 'I'm sorry. I'm so sorry, Vivian. You know that, right?'

Vivian nodded. She reached into her pocket and brought out the brown envelope. The prison officer looked over as Vivian handed it to David.

David raised an eyebrow, 'What's this?'

'You know,' Vivian replied.

David nodded slowly and took out the documents. 'Divorce papers.'

Vivian looked at him and he looked down at the table.

'Giving them to me in person?'

Vivian could feel her bottom lip trembling. She told herself to be strong, to put on her game face, as she did when at work.

'You always had more class than me.' David smiled and waved the thickset prison officer over.

The officer walked over and held out his hand. 'What's all this?' he asked, indicating the documents.

'You can read,' David replied, as he handed them over. He stood up and turned to Vivian. 'Goodbye, Viv.'

'Goodbye, David.' As Vivian watched him being led away by the prison officer, she wondered if – just as she did – he had a tear rolling down his cheek.

CALLUM, 2011

He was on his hands and knees. His blood was smeared on the white tiles beneath him. He saw another flash of blue as Tiny's boot connected with the side of his head. Callum had lost count of how many times he had attempted to scramble to his feet. He spat out a mix of phlegm and more blood that appeared bright red on top of the white tiles. There was a buzzing sound as Callum was struck with another blow.

He wasn't sure whether this came from a foot or a fist but he knew it didn't come from Tiny. It came from another inmate who now dragged him up from the ground. Callum stood there naked, dripping wet from his interrupted shower. He leaned against the inmate, who was holding him up.

'Jesus, you're heavy for a skinny fucker, aren't you?!' The inmate then punched Callum in his ribs. Callum crumpled to the ground once more and struggled to breathe.

'Don't worry Cal,' Tiny said, crouching over the naked mess on the floor. He laughed before saying, 'You'll be on the outside tomorrow, you'll be able to get a massage.'

'I say we give him one now,' Tiny's accomplice said, excited.

'Nah, we can save that for later, the motherfucker will probably be back. But in the meantime, I need my piggy bank looked after. So, like I said, make sure that pretty superstar brother of yours does what we've been speaking about and takes care of it.'

Callum lay on the cold tiles, breathing heavily, trying to appreciate the pause in the beating. He felt Tiny stroke his hair.

'Do you hear me? Everything will be okay for you both. Just make sure he looks after us the way we've looked after you in here, and the way we'll keep looking after you from tomorrow.' Tiny stood up and turned to his friend. 'Let's go.'

'Hold on.' The inmate continued looking down at Callum who had now managed to turn himself over, and was lying on his back. With a demonic expression, the inmate then straddled Callum and proceeded to slap him repeatedly.

Tiny looked on as the slaps became more frantic. He let the assault continue before dragging the inmate away.

'That's enough for now.'

The inmate stood up, his hands covered with Callum's blood, his mouth surrounded by spit.

Callum watched Tiny and the inmate wash their hands under the shower before walking away.

Lying on the ground and staring ahead, Callum thought about how many times Tiny had come to his aid during his sentence. He remembered all the stories he had heard about the big, allegedly gay gangster who had served all his adult life in jail. The 'deals' he had with prison officers, the drug and security empire he ran from inside. The people he had 'got rid of' for others.

Despite this severe beat down, Tiny was one of the few friends that Callum had, and he knew all too well that prisoners returning to the outside world needed friends more than ever.

KIERAN, TUESDAY 3 P.M.

'You must not blame yourself, Kieran.' Vivian watched her client continue to stare at the ground, slowly shaking his head. 'Your father has been coming to watch you play for years. This was just a tragic accident.'

Silence.

'I am so, so sorry.'

Kieran looked up at Vivian. 'That's why I have to make up for it.' Kieran began to nod. 'It's time I stopped neglecting my family.'

'I see. And how does Clarissa feel about your brother coming to stay with you?' Vivian leaned over her coffee table and poured Kieran a glass of water.

'Well … she says we'll talk about it when she's back from the tour.'

Vivian sat back on the sofa, crossed her legs and adjusted her fitted dark-blue blazer. She observed Kieran avoiding her eye contact again. 'She's back next week, isn't she?'

'Yeah.' Kieran cleared his throat nervously.

'But your brother is released tomorrow.'

Kieran sighed. 'Look, Clarissa doesn't want Callum to stay with me but it's not up to her.'

Vivian briefly wrote in her file then said, 'So you don't think it's fair that she has a say in who lives in the house you share.'

'It's my house,' Kieran declared, 'and I've had enough of people telling me what to do. I can make my own decisions. I'm a man, for fuck's sake.'

Kieran's outburst was met with silence. He was panting as Vivian calmly stared back at him. She gave a faint nod of her head before writing something down, and then she flicked back a few pages. 'You've been back in touch with Callum for almost a month?'

'Yeah,' Kieran replied. He unzipped his sports jacket. 'Since Dad's funeral. It's been … nice.

We've been talking about how things used to be, reminding each other about the fun we had when we were kids.' Kieran paused and looked down at his hands. 'Before all this.'

Vivian frowned. 'Before all what?'

'The money, and the cameras, and …' Kieran continued to look at his hands.

'Reconnecting with your brother has reminded you of growing up?'

Kieran looked up at Vivian and smiled. 'Yeah, it has.' He took a sip of water. 'It's been so nice talking to someone who knows me. Who doesn't want anything from me. Callum, me and my mum, we're going to—'

'So you don't think your brother wants anything from you?' Vivian interrupted.

Kieran put his glass down and rubbed his face before saying, 'No, I don't.' He looked into Vivian's eyes but could only hold her gaze for a second. Kieran shook his head. 'He never once asked me for anything while he was inside. I never visited him.'

'Kieran,' Vivian said in a soft voice, 'I can understand how tricky it must have been for someone in your position to visit somebody in prison.'

'That's no excuse,' Kieran said, shaking his head. 'He was there for me when we were kids. I wasn't there for him when he needed me. I owe him.' He looked at Vivian, sincerity etched on his face. 'I owe him, and there's nothing you, Clarissa, or Nathan can say about that.'

FREDDIE, 2011

Freddie stepped out of Lagos airport into the sweltering heat. Equipped with only a weekend bag, he shielded his eyes from the gleaming sun and headed over to a taxi rank.

'Dis way sah!' The man tugging at Freddie's arm was in his mid-thirties, he had a toothpick between his lips and he reached for Freddie's bag. As Freddie took a step back, holding onto his property, a dark-skinned older man shouted, 'Hey stupid! Don't jump the line! Get out!'

Freddie realised that the two men were cab drivers. He watched them argue over his custom.

'I will slap you now!' The older driver threatened the younger one.

Freddie found their exchange amusing, but after his long flight from Heathrow he was too tired to laugh. He reached into a pocket of his khaki trousers and pulled out a piece of paper. 'I'm trying to get to this place.' He held out the scribbled address.

Much to the younger driver's chagrin, the older man snatched it from Freddie's hand. He squinted and sucked his teeth. 'God, I can't read dis.' He then started to pat himself down. 'Where are my spectacles?' He became increasingly frustrated. 'God, where are dey?!'

The younger driver snatched the piece of paper. 'Ah, easy. Small, small journey.' He turned to Freddie with a huge smile. 'Follow me.'

Freddie obliged and headed to the driver's car, casting a look back to the older driver, who was still patting himself down, asking nobody in particular the whereabouts of his glasses.

Freddie was led to an old, battered grey BMW by the grinning driver. 'See, German car!' he said proudly.

Freddie frowned at the sight of the unsafe-looking vehicle. 'How long will the journey take?'

The driver scratched his shaved head, 'Forty-five minutes … two hours.'

'You mean forty-five minutes to an hour?' Freddie asked.

'Yes, yes. That's right!' The driver said, opening the door for Freddie.

Freddie regarded him sceptically before sitting in the back. The driver nodded and grinned at Freddie then hopped behind the wheel. He turned the key in the ignition but there was no result.

'Sorry mate,' Freddie said, looking at the driver fiddling with the key, 'if there's a problem I can just—'

'No problem!' the driver interrupted. He then said something in what Freddie recognised as Igbo but couldn't translate. The engine spluttered to life. 'Ah ha!' The driver beamed at Freddie through the rear-view mirror and they set off. Freddie felt around the black cracked leather seats of the car. He placed his bag beside him and tried to relax.

'England?' the driver asked in his thick accent.

'Sorry?'

'You from England?'

'Yes,' Freddie replied.

'London!' The driver shouted.

Freddie smiled and rolled down his window. The air was warm and unpleasant, and he could smell burning. He ran a hand across his sweaty forehead and lifted his arms. His armpits were soaked. 'Can you smell that?' Freddie asked the driver.

'I can't smell anything,' he replied, sounding annoyed.

'No I wasn't … I mean, can you smell burning?'

The driver grinned. 'This is Nigeria, man! We are hot people!' He then burst out laughing.

Freddie forced himself to join in.

'London, where they riot this year, isn't it?' The driver shook his head disapprovingly. 'How can they riot when they are rich? Stupid people! And they call it "Western Civilisation." Hmmm!'

Lost for words, Freddie locked eyes with the driver through the rear-view mirror.

The driver returned the stare and pointed to himself. 'Chidozie. What is your name?'

'Freddie.'

'Ehhh … first time in Nigeria?'

'I came here when I was a baby, so I don't remember much about it.'

Chidozie curled his lips downwards. 'You have small bag, so you don't come for wedding.'

Freddie looked at his weekend bag beside him. 'Oh, yes, it's a short trip.'

'But you can still bring present for your family, can you not?'

'I don't have much …' Freddie's voice faded as Chidozie mumbled something in Igbo. Feeling self-conscious and somewhat irritated, Freddie reclined in his seat.

After crawling away from the airport and slowly creeping through the chaotic traffic of the neighbouring area, the two men were now no longer boxed in by careless pedestrians and countless vehicles that seemed to contain drivers who were beeping their horns for fun. Freddie was sure that some of the cars he saw couldn't be road legal. In fact, the BMW in which he was currently a passenger now felt slightly safer (but only slightly).

They travelled across the bumpy road in silence for a while. Freddie unbuttoned his short-sleeved shirt almost all the way down. He looked out the window, squinting past the glaring sun, and watched the surroundings pass him by. He saw abandoned petrol stations and miles of dry grass. They passed a makeshift fruit stall. A small boy ran alongside the car holding out a dusty orange. Chidozie watched Freddie clumsily sift through his bag. He grabbed a handful of coins and just about managed to hand them to the boy. He declined the orange as he craned his neck out of the window to watch the boy scooping the coins up from the sand. Freddie leaned back in the seat and rubbed his moist face. He thought about his father. He became anxious as he tried to picture what his grave would look like. He began to question whether this was the right thing to do. Was it worth him flying more than six hours from London to visit the tombstone of a man whom he hadn't had any contact with for thirty years? A man that he only held a frozen, outdated image of?

Freddie thought about all the times that he would be on a bus and see an older black man. He would fantasise about one of these men being his father. He would dream that one day one of these men would turn around and say, 'I'm back, son.'

Freddie looked out at the now orangey sky. He glanced at his watch; they had been travelling for over an hour and a half. 'Are we close?'

'Yes, no problem,' Chidozie replied. He rested his right arm on the open window and steered with his left hand. 'So you visit family?'

Freddie ignored him and looked at the darkening sky.

'Freddie, you visit relatives?' Chidozie asked again.

Freddie continued to look out the window, and they passed yet another community of shack-like houses. 'I've come to bury my father.'

'Oh,' Chidozie said, and he spat his toothpick out the window. 'Funeral tomorrow?'

Freddie shook his head. 'No, he died almost two months ago.'

Chidozie curled his lips downwards again. 'Hmm ...'

'We weren't close,' said Freddie. 'He left me and my mother and sister thirty years ago.'

Chidozie and Freddie's eyes met through the rear-view mirror once more.

'We never saw him again.'

They rode on in silence for a little while before Chidozie said, 'Tarty years he left you?'

'Yes,' Freddie replied.

'And you come to visit his grave?'

Freddie didn't reply.

Chidozie nodded approvingly. 'You're a good man.'

VIVIAN

One of the Golden Rules of my job is: Do Not Get Emotionally Involved With Patients. Being a naturally emotional person, this is something that I have had to work on. I've found myself having to develop a Fifth Wall. It's quite a strange experience because my patients enjoy having someone to talk to. Although some of them show this more than others, the fact is they like having a person sat in front of them who they can express themselves to. A person who, by definition of their job, has to listen to them. And whether or not they like what I say to them in response to what they have told me, whether or not they feel uncomfortable when I note something down in their file, unless they are seeing me as part of Court Ordered treatment, they have each made a choice to be a patient.

So at first it felt like some sort of betrayal when I began to construct this Fifth Wall. The patient, me and their issues, remain safe within the four walls of the treatment room. And then the Fifth Wall maintains the line between our relationship becoming anything more than patient and therapist. As somebody who has been on the receiving end of the inevitable negativity that comes from a lack of communication, I have to admit that I never fail to note the discomfort I feel when I know that my natural, less professional opinion is to tell the person(s) sat in front of me to 'go to the police'. Or to 'get away from each other, your marriage will never work.' After all, I fought for my marriage longer than I should have. I ignored the writing on the wall.

Since many of my patients are in the public eye, I'd rather not have any outside influence – all I want to know about their lives is what they tell me. As a policy I do not have any newspapers or gossip magazines in my reception. I don't want my high-profile patients thinking that there is any chance of bias in my office. And I don't want my patients who suffer from body image issues, or identity issues, having a magazine in front of them that dictates how we should think, what we should wear, and how we should define beauty.

Unfortunately, every so often I come across something about some of my famous clients, past or present. The death of Gemma and Pete is by far the most tragic of all. It was one thing imagining what the papers would make of the death of Kieran's father, but that was only after I had heard about it directly from Kieran. And I then made an even more conscious effort to avoid the press and internet. But the fact that Gemma and Pete were actual patients of mine is something that I know will take a long time for me to get over. The feelings of regret that I was overcome with when their deaths were brought to my attention by my assistant is something that I'm going to have to compartmentalise – another 'skill' one has to develop in my field.

Perhaps the fact that they were outpatients at the time the dreadful tragedy struck is something I have been attempting to seek comfort from. Gemma's tardiness and then eventual absences made it more and more difficult to treat them. Some patients remain patients for what seems like forever, coming back every single week, as if therapy is a routine etched into their lives indefinitely. Some people appear to operate under a self-imposed discipline of coming in for a period of three to six months each year. Some people completely disappear after one or two sessions – it's become easier for me to be able to predict which particular patient is going to fall into which particular category. One thing I could not foresee was the apparent suicide–murder of Gemma and Pete. Yes, it was clear to me very early on that their marriage was doomed. To me, this was an obvious case of two people who had fallen in love very young and had built a relationship based on the fantasies of their youth. They were clearly hanging on to the feelings that were induced by the dreams that they shared at the start of their romance. Being with somebody for half of your life is always going to be a challenge. People grow (perhaps slowly in Pete's case) and evolve. In an ideal world lovers would grow and evolve together, enjoying and embracing each other's new findings, all the while not stunting each other's growth. But I saw no sign of this with Gemma and Pete. When Pete's ambition, the very thing which drew Gemma to him in the first place, began to return – albeit slowly – Gemma became jealous. She had clearly become used to him being down and out. And because she was unfulfilled in their marriage (dreams not panning out exactly how they had fantasised) she developed a love-hate relationship with her role as her husband's rock. And although I feel the catalyst for her infidelity was that of the neglect she felt as Pete continued to put the majority of his energy into chasing his dreams, and initially being an attempt to regain his attention, I also believe it was an abuse of her power. Gemma knew Pete wasn't going to leave her, especially while his confidence was at rock bottom. Especially when he was unemployed. He needed her. And I think that when one partner feels that the other needs them more than vice versa, there's trouble ahead. My ex-husband thought that I would never leave – and who could blame him? If you hit somebody, and there are no ramifications, how are you supposed to be deterred? Especially if that person accepts the role of superwoman, as I did in my case. I knew that David regretted it after every single time he hit me. But I also know that I enabled him to justify it to himself by my accepting the role of Mrs Invincible. The rock on which her damaged husband could lean on. Another thing I know is that it is not always easy to do what you know is the right thing. In Gemma and Pete's case, I think the right thing would have been for them to pursue separate lives. They were not twenty years old anymore – an age period where it's possibly more common to try and get your partners attention by sleeping around. A time in your life where you can take more gambles, and have less responsibility for your actions.

I always rooted for David, and I like to think that my ex-husband now knows that. I think Gemma stopped rooting for Pete, and maybe Pete knew this. And now they're both dead I ask myself why didn't he leave her? Perhaps he still loved her, or maybe he was in love with the idea of them.

Was he possibly being driven by the promise of looking after her? A promise that it was clear Gemma held him to? He was clearly broken, but I saw a determination in him. Pete had to be determined to persevere in what strikes me as an incredibly difficult and fickle industry. He had to be determined to turn up on time to every single session of marriage counselling, whether or not his wife was present. And if Gemma was so unhappy, why didn't she leave Pete? But again, sometimes it's hard to do what you know is the right thing.

I try to treat my patients as individuals, but I give a slight variation to the rules when I'm treating couples. I try to group their individual problems into one category and see if we can deal with what I call an 'Amalgamated Problem'. This is not always successful; in Gemma and Pete's case it clearly failed, and I'm currently struggling to deal with this. As a couple I do not believe that Gemma and Pete could be helped. But as individuals I think things could have been different, especially in Pete's case. Some of my friends think that my job is linked to some sort of ability to read people's minds, and as absurd as it sounds, to somehow predict the future. Obviously this isn't the case but there are times when I notice certain mirroring patterns in specific personalities.

One moment I tell myself that there is nothing I could have done to prevent what happened between Gemma and Pete, but every other second I ask myself why I didn't look out for any signs. In hindsight, I would have thought that, if anything, maybe Gemma would have done something to hurt herself. I am trying to convince myself that this thought couldn't have been that strong because if it was I would have urged Gemma to see me separately. Suicide that is linked to seeking attention is quite specific, and as a side note I'm happy to say that I think I'm making progress with the sixteen-year-old girl I've been treating for the past few months.

For me the hardest and most frustrating thing about my job is the fact that I'm constantly having to question my judgement: patient confidentiality is an absolute. Therefore, unless a patient tells me that they are going to kill somebody, I cannot disclose anything that is said inside the four walls of my treatment room to anybody else. Even in the event of a patient telling me that they are going to kill someone, I would only be able to alert the particular person at risk, and only that person. I would then hope that the potential victim would then inform the police. I cannot even go to the police if a patient tells me that they are living in fear for their own life. All I can do is urge them to go to the police themselves. All this while making a judgement as to who is crying a little louder for help and who is being deadly serious.

Not all patients can be helped, and although Gemma and Pete had discharged themselves, it's currently very difficult for me to not look upon that particular chapter as at least a little bit of a failure on my part.

Vivian slowly closed her diary and placed it along with her pen in the top drawer of her bedside table. She switched off the lamp and looked at the digital alarm clock. In front of the backdrop of her dark bedroom the illuminated red figures told her it was 3.16 a.m.

She stared at the numerals and thought about how having her diary away from her office was a risk, and she made a mental note to return it to the safe behind her bookshelf as soon as she got into work. She then tried to ignore the craving for red wine that was beginning to creep into her thoughts. Vivian's attempt to chase the invading craving only led her back to wondering if she could have done anything differently to help Gemma and Pete.

The next time she looked at her alarm clock the display read 3.48 a.m. She forced herself to smile and recalled her motto about hope: *I stayed with David because I hoped that we could get past our problems. In hindsight maybe that was blind hope. But what would get me out of bed each morning if I didn't have hope? And ultimately, if I didn't have hope – no matter how delusional – if I didn't make an effort to look on the bright side and attempt to see the good in people, what the hell would be the point of my job?*

As she lay back and shut her eyes, she silently reminded herself, *Fifth Wall, Vivian. Fifth Wall.*

KIERAN, 2011

'I'm so sorry, Mum.' Kieran and Anna sat at her dining table, crying as they embraced one another. 'If Dad hadn't driven to see the game—'

'Shush,' Anna interrupted Kieran, 'stop it.'

'But it's my fault.'

Anna grabbed Kieran by the shoulders. 'No it isn't. You stop that, right now. You hear me? Right now.' She ran her thumb across his cheek, smearing his tears.

Kieran dipped his head slightly. The two of them sat in the small family kitchen, the aroma of the room taking Kieran back to when he was a child. He embraced his mother once more, and closed his eyes as he recalled the countless times he would be sat in this exact position after school. Crying into her chest after a day of ridicule. Kieran was bigger now, stronger, rich and famous. Anna was small and frail but she still made Kieran feel safe.

'Now,' said Anna, 'have you eaten?'

'I'm not hungry, Mum.'

'Come on honey, you've just been at training. Let me make you that post-game pasta you always used to like.'

Kieran smiled at the memory as Anna went over to the kitchen cupboard. He noticed how tiny she was as she hunted for ingredients. 'Mum, you need to eat something too. Your weight's dropped a lot.'

She waved a dismissive hand in his direction.

Kieran looked around the kitchen, his mind beginning to conjure up translucent images of the past. He saw his father sat across from him, reading the Sunday paper. Callum appeared, covered in flour as he and Kieran helped their mother bake a cake. He pictured himself on his hands and knees, scrubbing the kitchen floor, desperately trying to clean the mud left by his football boots before his mum caught him.

Kieran went over to his mother at the counter. 'Callum's coming to stay with me tomorrow.'

Anna stopped what she was doing, shut her eyes tightly, and placed both hands on the counter. The drip of the tap was the only sound in the room until she spoke.

'No.'

'Mum,' Callum said quietly.

'No!' Anna screamed, before grabbing a plate and throwing it against a wall.

Kieran ducked as it smashed. He wrapped his arms around his mother's diminutive frame. 'Mum, what are you doing?'

He tried to hold her steady as she trembled in his grip. 'Mum?' he said, watching her shiver. 'Come over here, sit down.' He guided her back to the dining table. 'I'll put the kettle on.'

Anna grabbed his wrist before he moved off. 'Kieran, I don't want Callum anywhere near you.'

'Don't, Mum.' Kieran tried to release himself from her surprisingly strong grip.

'He's trouble, Kieran. I don't want him getting you into trouble.'

'We're not kids anymore, Mum—'

Anna banged her pale fist against the table. 'He hasn't changed! Being bad is all he knows. Please, Kieran.'

Kieran looked at his mother becoming increasingly worked up, and he thought about how much she had aged recently. 'You're going to give yourself a heart attack—'

'You're giving me a heart attack!' she shouted. 'Do you know how hard we worked to make sure that you didn't end up like him?'

'Mum, he needs—'

'Think of your father, for Christ's sake!'

Kieran rubbed his face and unzipped his tracksuit top, his mother's last statement ringing in his head.

'He's my brother. We need to be there for him.' Kieran sat down next to Anna. 'I've never visited him once.'

'You couldn't!'

'No, Mum, I don't want to make any more excuses.'

Anna got up and walked back over to the kitchen counter. Kieran followed her.

'Mum, at the funeral Callum said something about sending me letters.'

Anna didn't respond, instead choosing to busy herself with the pots and pans.

'I was thinking that he was making it up,' Kieran continued. 'He doesn't have my address.' He watched his mother, continuing to ignore him. 'But then I was thinking that maybe he sent the letters here.'

Anna aggressively stirred a pot of pasta over the hob. Kieran bit his bottom lip as he watched her, anger growing inside of him.

'Where are the letters, Mum?'

Anna continued to ignore her son.

'Where are the letters?' Kieran asked once more, not attempting to conceal his fury. 'Where are the letters?'

'I threw them out!' Anna yelled at the top of her voice. 'I destroyed them! I don't want him anywhere near you!'

Kieran caught her just before she collapsed to the ground. He held her tiny body tight, and they both sunk to the floor, crying in each other's arms.

FREDDIE, 2011

This time Freddie sat next to Chidozie in the front of the car. It was a bright morning and the men were back on the road having stopped at Chidozie's home for the night.

'Your wife is a great cook,' Freddie said, as the breeze ran over his face through the open window. For some reason the air felt better today.

'Ah!' Chidozie exclaimed. 'That was nothing! Had she known that we were going to have a guest, hey!' – he tapped the steering wheel in delight – 'you would have thought you were in heaven!'

Freddie joined in with Chidozie's laughter.

'I'm telling you!' Chidozie went on. 'She's famously known as the best cook in the compound!'

Freddie smiled. 'I believe you!'

The day before, once it had become too dark, Chidozie had suggested that they head towards his home and stop off for the night. The roads were badly lit, and Freddie hadn't anticipated the drive to his father's grave to have taken so long. It occurred to him how little he had planned this trip. He simply wanted to visit his father's gravesite, then perhaps get a hotel for the night, before flying back to London the next day. He had made tentative plans to stay with a distant uncle for the night but this hadn't appealed to him. Dining with Chidozie, his wife and young son, had illustrated to Freddie how detached he was from the country of his parents' birth. It was as if his connection to Nigeria had ended the day his father had absconded from the family.

Chidozie's home was modest, and it was only this morning that Freddie had got to see it properly. When they had arrived last night, the village had suffered a power cut. Freddie was surprised at the nonchalance with which Chidozie had dealt with the situation. 'Okay, no problem,' he had said to a neighbour who had greeted them on their arrival. 'Have you put fuel in the generator?'

'We're doing it now, Uncle,' the boy, who looked about twelve years old, had replied.

'Oh ya, hurry up,' Chidozie said, gesturing to the other side of the compound.

The boy briefly glanced at Freddie before running off.

Chidozie smiled at Freddie, and his teeth and eyes were bright white against the darkness. Freddie followed behind as Chidozie led him to a small house.

'Welcome to my home,' he grinned at Freddie as he unlocked the iron gate.

When they entered, Freddie was immediately hit by a spicy smell. He blinked the tears away that had suddenly welled up in his eyes. He squinted through the darkness as a figure holding a torch came towards him. Once the figure had come closer, Freddie could see it was a woman. She was holding a small boy in her other arm. She kissed Chidozie, and he took the child from her.

'This is Freddie, my English friend!' Chidozie said, flicking his head towards Freddie.

The woman nodded. 'You are welcome.'

'Hello,' Freddie replied. 'Pleased to meet you.'

Chidozie pointed towards the woman with his spare hand. 'This is my wife, Gold.'

'That's a nice name,' Freddie said politely.

The lights suddenly flickered on.

'Ah!' Chidozie beamed, 'the generator!'

The room was only lit to a dim glow but Freddie saw Chidozie's wife's features for the first time, and her beauty took him aback. She appeared to be in her twenties and she wore a brown gele on her head. This was teamed with a matching brown buba and iro, which were wrapped around her slender frame.

Freddie smiled at her.

'And this is my boy!' Chidozie announced proudly.

Freddie looked at the cute dark-skinned child. He was smiling and seemed to cheer at his father's introduction. 'He's going to play football when he is big.'

'Really?' Freddie smiled at the child. 'You like football?'

The boy nodded.

Freddie turned to Chidozie. 'He's beautiful.'

Chidozie grinned and spoke to his wife in Igbo.

When Gold left the compact, neatly decorated room, Chidozie said, 'Are you hungry? My wife has prepared some food.' He wandered towards the small dining table in the corner. 'Come on, please, sit.'

Freddie joined Chidozie at the table. He held out his arms. 'May I?'

Chidozie smiled and handed his son over to Freddie.

'What's his name?' Freddie asked, bouncing the happy boy on his lap.

'Godswill,' Chidozie replied. 'He's almost three years old.'

They sat in silence as Freddie rocked the child. After a moment, Freddie asked, 'Why didn't you tell me that the journey was going to take all day?'

'Well,' Chidozie stretched in his chair, 'that would have been bad for business wouldn't it?'

Freddie frowned.

'Would you not have sought alternative transportation if I told you the distance?'

'There was no need for you lie to me.'

'No lie! The roads are bad. It really should take two hours if the government fixed our roads.'

Freddie shook his head. 'There must have been a quicker way.'

'No. Bus, coach, the same. Our roads are bad. So why let them take the money, eh?' Chidozie smiled cheekily. 'I am going to make a lot of money from this!'

'Hang on a minute—'

'Don't worry …' Chidozie interrupted, 'I make good price. And look …' he pointed at his wife walking towards them with plates of food. 'You get free meal!'

Freddie chuckled incredulously. 'I don't even know you.'

'Hey,' Chidozie said, taking a sip of the Supermalt that his wife had also placed on the table, 'you are Nigerian aren't you?'

'Yes but—'

'So you are my brother,' Chidozie cut in.

Gold returned with a plate for herself, took Godswill from Freddie and joined the men at the table.

'Anyway,' Chidozie spoke with a mouthful of egusi, 'I should be worried about you. I hope you don't think it's okay to riot here.' Chidozie laughed and his wife joined in. Godswill squealed, and Freddie was shocked and amused by his audacity.

'Come on, eat!'

As Freddie tucked in, the lights cut out again.

KIERAN, 2011

'Baby, please don't bail on me at the last minute again.' Clarissa flicked a stray lock of her brown extensions away from her face.

Kieran looked at his fiancée sitting across from him. He thought about how he had seen her in magazines more times than he had seen her in the flesh lately.

He thought about how she was turning more and more into a moving image of all the pictures spread across the glossy tabloids. An all-dancing, all-singing fantasy figure. Every day it became harder for Kieran to see past the St Tropez tan, topped up by Clarissa's recent trip to Spain on the final leg of Girl-Fiends' European tour.

Somewhere behind the expensive hair and fake eyelashes was the girl he had fallen in love with as a teenager. Somewhere behind those big green eyes that were currently staring down at her engagement ring, was Clarissa Harvey.

Kieran had just turned sixteen and was about to sign his first contract as a professional football player. He was living with Nathan in a serviced apartment provided by the club. On his way to and from training he would see four cute girls getting in and out of a minivan. He immediately knew that he liked Clarissa, and Nathan knew this too. She was the most beautiful girl he had ever seen. Kieran knew that Nathan would be wary, and that there was no way he was going to let some silly crush on a girl distract the young prodigy. Whenever their paths would cross, Kieran could see how irritated Nathan would become. He could imagine his

mentors' mind going into overtime: *'... come on son, focus. We've come this far.*
I'll be damned if all my ... I mean our, hard work is going to be usurped by puppy
love." Kieran knew that Nathan hoped his shyness would get the better of him,
and perhaps this made him more determined to talk to Clarissa.

One evening, Kieran and Nathan were having dinner at an Italian restaurant
near the apartments. All night, Kieran couldn't keep his eyes off the table in the
corner, the one occupied by Clarissa and her three female companions. Also at
the table with the girls was a man in his late thirties that Kieran noticed always
wore black.

Kieran also noticed that the man's expression seemed to turn from friendly to
sour every time their eyes met.

'Meet me at the car park in five minutes.'

Kieran had thought he was dreaming when the beautiful girl said this to him. He
was on the way back from the toilet, and she had appeared out of nowhere.

'Give me your phone.' Kieran didn't say anything. He simply obliged, wearing a
nervous expression as he handed it over. She smiled, apparently enjoying the
hold she had over him.

'My name's Clarissa,' she said.

Kieran watched her punching the keypad. He thought she looked like a
mermaid. Her hair was long and brown. She wore large gold hoops in each ear,
and a short green dress, with a denim jacket over it. She smelt incredible. He was
in love.

'Kieran, innit?' Clarissa said, handing the phone back over.

'Errm, yeah … how did you …?' Kieran's voice faded, extinguished by shyness.

'I have my ways.' Clarissa smiled at him, and he was sure that she had descended from heaven. 'Okay, I have to go.' She peered round the corner. 'Text me when you get back, okay?'

Kieran nodded.

That night Kieran and Clarissa had their first kiss, and she became Kieran's first and only love.

He learned that she was in a girl band called Sauce Kittens, and that their sour-faced, all-black-wearing manager had plans for them to take over the world. She learned that he had just turned pro. And they both learned how to love.
Kieran wished that they could both learn all over again. Somewhere in the maze of fame and fortune, that part of them had been lost. It had been pushed to the limit by countless allegations of his infidelity, her eating disorders and breakdowns due to 'exhaustion', the scrutiny and the time spent apart. This was their relationship.

They had nothing to talk about. Clarissa and Kieran communicated through celluloid. They may as well have been strangers reading about each other's lives.

Sunday lunch at their local chic gastropub was their attempt at holding on to the glory days. But once in the last nine weeks wasn't good enough, and they both knew it.

Kieran took a bite of his pasta. 'Why can't we just stay at home for once?'

'Because we have to celebrate being number one.'

Kieran adjusted his dark shades on the bridge of his nose. 'So let's celebrate at home.'

'The label won't be happy, babe.' Clarissa's large green eyes welled up. 'Please, people are starting to talk.'

Kieran could feel himself getting angry and he looked at her. She picked her sunglasses up from the table and put them on, as if wanting to stop his gaze penetrating any further.

'Who are these fucking "people"? That's all you ever say – "people". Fuck.' Kieran's voice became louder with each sentence. 'Why can't it ever be just us?'

'Kieran, please ...' Clarissa said, throwing quick glances over both shoulders, 'people are staring.'

'Fuck!' Kieran shouted.

Just then his mobile phone rang. He looked at the screen which read *Unknown Number*. He frowned and cancelled the call.

'Who was that?' Clarissa asked, dabbing the tear that sneaked out from under her shades. 'One of your hoes?'

'I don't know who it was.'

'Yeah, fucking right.' Clarissa began to sob. 'I hate you, I fucking hate you.'

Kieran looked around the heated patio, and indeed, their fellow al fresco diners were staring. He lowered his head, and his phone rang again. He showed Clarissa the screen.

'See, it's a blocked number. I don't know who it is.'

Clarissa ignored him and took a sip of water.

Kieran put the handset to his ear. 'Who's this?'

'Your friend.'

'I haven't got time for this shit.' Kieran hung up. He looked at Clarissa who had now turned her body to the side, demonstrating that she was going to be ignoring him.

'How many times do I have to change my flipping number?'

Clarissa said nothing. Kieran shook his head and signalled for the waitress to come over.

'Would you like the bill, Mr Ledley?' The pretty, dark-haired woman asked, leaning a little closer to Kieran than Clarissa appreciated.

'Yes, we would,' said Clarissa.

The waitress stood there, unimpressed by Clarissa's tone.

'Well, do you mind?' Clarissa waved a dismissive hand towards her, making sure it was the hand on which her engagement ring lived. 'We're in a bit of a rush.'

The waitress cleared her throat and wore a false smile. 'Certainly.'

'Slut,' Clarissa said, looking in the direction of the departing waitress.

Kieran's phone rang again.

'Seriously, who the fuck is that?' Clarissa asked. She removed her sunglasses and revealed her slightly smudged mascara.

'I don't know.' Kieran clenched his jaw. He looked back at Clarissa's green eyes and put the phone to his ear. 'Who the fuck is this?'

'It's not nice to make your fiancée cry.' Kieran didn't recognise the relaxed, precise voice on the phone at all.

'What?'

'Why would you make such a beautiful girl cry?'

'What are you talking about?'

'Why can't you just enjoy your pasta, eh?'

Kieran slowly looked from side to side. 'Who the fuck is this?'

'I already told you, a friend.'

The waitress returned with the bill, gave Clarissa a dirty look, and walked away.

'That waitress is very pretty isn't she? Not as pretty as Clarissa, though.'

Kieran stood up, his eyes darting around the patio. 'Who the fuck is this?!'

'Sit down, don't make a scene.' The voice on the phone remained calm.

'Kieran, what the hell is wrong with you?' Clarissa asked.

Kieran looked at the fellow diners, who were getting more and more irritated with his behaviour. He sat down.

'Look at Clarissa, sitting there in her purple maxi dress. It really brings out the colour of her eyes ... Oooh, the winter sun is obviously making her a little thirsty.'

Kieran felt dizzy as he looked at his fiancée, in her purple maxi dress, taking a sip of water.

'Now you listen to me carefully, pretty boy. We need twenty thousand pounds by midday on Friday, or you won't be getting married.'

The line went dead, and Kieran put the phone on the table.

'Kieran, what the fuck is wrong with you?' a confused Clarissa asked, as she adjusted her purple dress.

Kieran continued to scan the bushes. He remembered the man who'd confronted him outside Vivian's office. He found himself expecting him to appear.

He then thought back to the voice on the phone and tried to remember if it sounded like the desperate man at the car park. Kieran didn't think it did.

'What are you staring at?' an irritated Clarissa asked.

Kieran blinked and looked towards his fiancée. Even though his brother's release had been delayed due to a fight with another inmate, now didn't seem like the best time for him to mention that Callum was coming to stay with them.

FREDDIE, 2011

As they drove, Freddie reflected on the night at Chidozie's house. He tried to remember the last time he had felt so free and anonymous. He had been moved by the affection Chidozie showed his wife and child, by how simply they appeared to live. Their possessions were basic but they seemed so happy. This morning, on the way to the car, Chidozie had been continuously stopped and greeted by his neighbours. He was clearly very popular and he politely introduced Freddie as his 'English friend'. Freddie laughed when he recalled Chidozie's attempt at an English accent.

They had bonded over dinner. Freddie had told them about Carol, Theo and Alfie. When he showed them pictures of his family on his phone, Chidozie had said, 'They are white but you must one day bring them to your country.' He then smiled and promised that his wife would cook an even better meal for them when they came to visit.

When he immediately began speaking to Gold in Igbo, Freddie thought that perhaps they had already started to organise the hypothetical visit.

Freddie had told them about his job, and he had tried to convince Chidozie that the London riots were a rare outrage. He remembered how confused Chidozie had been when he tried to explain that the shooting of an unarmed man had sparked the whole thing off.

'Why they shoot him?' Chidozie asked, shaking his head furiously. 'I don't understand, why, why?' Chidozie was further disgusted when Freddie said that he and the residents of Woundham still didn't know the answer.

'We are almost there,' Chidozie said as he steered the car around a bumpy bend.

Freddie's heart missed a beat. 'Are you sure?'

Chidozie gave his softest smile yet. 'I promise this time.'

They drove on for a few minutes as Freddie remembered why he had made this trip. He was awash with nerves as they slowly entered what appeared to be a small makeshift cemetery in the corner of a village. The men stepped out of the vehicle and Freddie looked around the unremarkable, deserted area. Chidozie looked at the crumpled address in his hand.

'This is definitely the place.'

They walked towards a cluster of large rocks. There was one with 'FRANK CHIKA ABANI' carved on it.

'That's it,' Freddie said. He took in the dates and they matched up. He bowed his head and looked down at his sand-covered toes poking out of his dusty sandals.

Tears welled in Freddie's eyes. He knelt down and placed a hand on the improvised tomb. When he closed his eyes he felt Chidozie put a hand on his shoulder. Freddie touched Chidozie's hand in acknowledgement.

After a deep breath Freddie stood up and said, 'Okay.'

Chidozie patted Freddie's back and walked him back to the car.

As Chidozie put the battered BMW into gear and turned the vehicle around, Freddie watched the tombstone shrink in size through the rear-view mirror.

You have nothing to prove. Freddie had never believed this so much.

CALLUM, 2011

Callum rubbed his stomach and lay back on the enormous, white L-shaped leather sofa. It was immaculate, as if it had never been sat on. With the white walls and marble floors, he could have been in heaven. This would have been complete paradise for him had he not just received a message from Tiny, reminding him of their 'arrangement'. On his release, Tiny had provided him with a mobile phone so they could 'keep in touch'. And Callum had just received his first 'courtesy text' that read: *10% a week from pretty boy. Don't play with me. In the meantime, hav a drink 4 me on the other side :)*

Callum wasn't smiling as he looked around the room. Next to half a bottle of whisky there was a large bowl of cereal on the thick black wooden table in front of the sofa. An empty bottle of red wine rolled back and forth slightly, tipped on its side on the floor, and there was a large oily box of pizza by Callum's legs.

He pocketed his phone as he tried to block out the message, and listened to the soundtrack of sexual pleasure coming from the sixty-inch flatscreen television hanging on the wall. Callum stared at the high ceiling and wondered when the last time he watched porn had been. He tried to recall the last time he had eaten a pizza, or drank alcohol. The now free Callum hadn't been in an open space, without supervision, for over two years, and he had certainly never been in a place as big or as nice as this in his entire life.

'Wow,' he said to himself, sitting up in awe of the mansion. 'Little bro's done good.' He picked up the bottle of whisky from the table and took a swig.

He tried to stand up and laughed when his legs gave way. He looked at the plasma screen and gawped at the tangled bodies performing sex acts on one another.

Callum attempted to get to his feet once more, succeeding this time. Keeping his eyes on the large screen, he made his way towards the stairs. He stumbled and quickly regained his balance, laughing again, then finally managed to get to the top of the stairs.

Callum wanted to enjoy being all alone in Kieran's house but he couldn't forget Tiny's message. His freedom was burdened by the beating that he had received in the shower before his release. Scraps were nothing new to Callum. He had been in an incalculable number during his various prison sentences. Despite his thinning frame, while inside he kept up his role as a fighter, taking on all comers, just like when he was at school. Winning, losing, and earning some respect along the way.

However, he wasn't everybody's cup of tea, and there were only so many times he could be warned by prison guards that he would 'eventually get what was coming' to him. So when Tiny opened his arms and said that he'd make sure he was looked after, Callum thought only a fool wouldn't align himself with the big 'lifer'. Yes he would soon be called 'Tiny's Bitch', and rumours abounded that he was one of Tiny's 'Boy Toys'. But Callum didn't let that dissuade him.

As his sentence was coming to an end, it didn't take long for Callum to realise that he was about to begin another one.

Tiny may have been serving two life sentences for murder, but Callum knew that he was indebted to him for the rest of his life. He knew he had to find a way to get Kieran to part with money on a weekly basis.

He thought about the opulence he had experienced in the very short time he had been in Kieran's world. He asked himself whether twenty thousand pounds a week was small change to his stepbrother? Maybe he could just tell him the truth and ask him for the cash? After all, he'd looked after his little brother when they were kids. Who knows? Kieran could have been seriously hurt growing up, if it hadn't been for him. *Without me*, Callum convinced himself, *Kieran might not have made it as a football player*. A bout of anger shot up Callum's spine as he remembered their contrasting childhoods.

He was going to get the money from Kieran, and he was going to start by stealing.

He went into his stepbrother's large bedroom. He took in the neatly made four-poster bed, its perfectly folded white sheets making it look hardly slept in.

He began to search through the drawers, pausing when he found Clarissa's underwear. Callum stood still, slowly caressing Clarissa's lingerie as he recalled how he used to masturbate to his little brother's fiancée's sexy magazine pictures when he was in prison. He suddenly awoke from his trance and began frantically going through the rest of the drawers. Once they were all tipped out, he entered the large walk-in wardrobe in the corner of the room. On entering, Callum was greeted by the smell of leather mixed with cologne and some sort of perfume. Kieran's suits lined one side of the wall, with his shoes and trainers underneath.

The other side of the room was symmetrically decorated with Clarissa's outfits and shoes. There was a drawer in the middle of the huge wardrobe which had sunglasses and jewellery on top of it. Scanning the room, Callum tried to estimate how much all the items were worth. He went over to Clarissa's side of the wardrobe, running his fingers down her dresses. From the corner of his eye he spotted a black shoebox. He smiled when he discovered what was inside. Callum slid his tracksuit bottoms down to his ankles, and began to masturbate as he held a naked picture of Clarissa out in front of him. Keeping his eyes fixed on Clarissa's face he brought himself to a climax.

His heart pounding, and panting ever so slightly, he went through the rest of the pictures and discovered four more nude shots of Clarissa. Callum remained standing there with his tracksuit bottoms around his ankles. He had an idea.

KIERAN AND CLARISSA, 2011

Kieran kissed Clarissa on her forehead. 'Stop crying, babe. We'll sort this.'

Clarissa was sat in between Kieran and her publicist, Louise. She buried her head into Kieran's chest, and her shoulders heaved as her wailing echoed throughout the large house.

'How are we going to sort it?!' she shrieked. 'How?!'

Kieran shook his head, lost for words.

Louise rubbed Clarissa's back. 'We always do, okay?' She grabbed Clarissa's face with both hands. 'You know we do.'

Kieran's eyebrows knitted together. He'd never really liked Louise. He always found the short woman a little dramatic and thought that this influenced Clarissa's behaviour. He was also irked by the way she tried to dress younger than her forty-two years. As far as he was concerned, Louise enjoyed a scandal and the opportunity to be a heroine.

'Fucking get rid of them!' Clarissa screamed, apparently spurred on by Louise's theatrics. She then swept the tabloids off the large coffee table in front of them. 'POP STAR IN NAKED SNAPS SCANDAL' said one red top. 'BIRTHDAY SHOOT' read another, and in a nod to Girl-Fiends' most recent single, 'U R So Rude', 'U R SO NUDE' announced one glossy.

Clarissa had returned home from the final leg of her band's European tour to find that her naked form was all over the newspapers. It was the press's wet dream: the country's most photographed pop star, one half of glamour couple 'Kier-Rissa' in all her glory.

Nathan made his way over from the kitchen with a cup of coffee. He placed it in front of Clarissa. 'Here you go, darling.'

Louise eyed Nathan and the cup suspiciously.

'No sugar, just as you asked,' Nathan said with a smile.

Clarissa blew her nose before taking a sip. 'Thanks.' She looked at Kieran. 'I just don't understand how these could have got out.'

'I really don't get it,' Kieran replied, adjusting his tear-soaked T-shirt.

'Have you had any builders round lately?' Louise asked.

'You haven't, have you?' Nathan answered on Kieran's behalf. 'I mean, we're always careful with things like that. We always use the same people, and we make sure that they sign confidentiality agreements.'

'Yes,' Louise said, standing up. She walked to the centre of the room and began to pace up and down, like a detective. 'But you can never be too careful.' She looked from Nathan to Kieran, before turning to Clarissa. 'There is a mole in this room.'

'Hang on a second. Calm down,' Kieran said from the sofa. 'Don't be so ridiculous. There is no "mole" here.'

Louise continued to look at Clarissa. 'You see,' she said in a raised voice, gesturing towards Kieran. 'I've warned you many times before, he is too trusting.'

'What are you talking about?!' Kieran demanded, rising from the sofa.

'He has too many people around him!' Louise appealed to Clarissa, ignoring Kieran.

'Now you just hang on,' Nathan chimed in.

'Don't talk to me like that!' Louise said, pointing at Nathan.

'Like what?!' Nathan asked, exasperated.

Louise continued. 'I know all about you shady agents. Who knows what you're involved in?!'

Nathan took a few steps towards Louise, the contrast of her short frame and his large build even more apparent. 'Don't you ever accuse me of anything, you stupid bitch!'

'Fuck you, you fat bastard!'

Clarissa continued to sob and Kieran attempted to interject. 'This really isn't helping—'

'No!' Nathan bellowed. 'How do we know that you didn't plant the photos yourself? You publicity hungry—'

'I am not publicity hungry!' Clarissa shrieked in between tears. 'It's all about the music!'

'Not you, sweetheart,' Nathan replied in an irritated tone. He flicked his head towards Louise, 'Miss Judgemental over there!'

Louise clutched her chest. 'How dare you?' She lowered her voice. 'How dare you accuse me of something so cheap?' She raised it again. 'How dare you?!'

Just then, the toilet could be heard flushing from the other side of the landing. In walked Callum drying his wet hands on one of Kieran's shirts.

'Alright guys? What's all the commotion?' He looked at the four of them frozen in each of their spots: Clarissa on the sofa, Kieran standing beside her, and Nathan and Louise taking a break from squaring up to one another.

Nathan turned to Kieran. 'What the fuck is he doing here?'

'I thought we agreed that he was going to stay with your mum,' Clarissa said, blinking furiously, her bloodshot eyes becoming redder by the second.

'Yeah,' Kieran replied quietly, 'we're just …'

Nathan's mouth hung open. 'Son, what the hell is going on?'

Kieran puffed out his cheeks and headed over to Callum. 'Cal, go upstairs for a little bit, yeah?'

'Why?'

'Please, just go,' Kieran replied, just about managing to keep his voice down. 'I'll see you in a sec.'

Callum looked towards them all before trudging up the stairs, expressionless.

As Kieran headed back towards the lounge, Clarissa leapt up from the sofa and began swinging her arms towards him.

'You prick! You promised! What the fuck is that criminal doing in our house?!'

'Babe!' Kieran called out as he tried to fend off the attack.

Louise restrained her. 'Honey, stop it. Breathe, honey, just breathe.'

It was now Nathan's turn to play peacemaker. 'Clarissa, take it easy, darling.' He stepped in between her and Kieran. 'Son. Think very carefully about what you're doing. This is not a good idea.'

Clarissa collapsed onto the sofa. 'It was him! The pervert! He's sick! Oh my God!' Her second round of crying began.

'Breathe, honey, that's it.'

Kieran looked at the short Louise, playing mummy to his fiancée. He saw Nathan shaking his head towards him. Kieran spoke. 'We have no proof.'

Nathan grabbed him by the shoulders. 'Son, listen to me. Callum needs to be as far away from you as possible.'

'It's just like when we were kids all over again,' Kieran replied, shaking him off.

'Kieran, don't do this,' Nathan said, rubbing his temples.

'"Stay away from him, he's a bad influence",' Kieran continued, mocking Nathan's words from his past. '"Kieran has so much potential, Mr Ledley. I just hope that Callum doesn't jeopardise things for him."' Kieran clenched his fists and strode over to the side table.

'Oh grow up, Kieran!' Clarissa screamed from the sofa.

'Exactly! I am grown-up. I'm a man. I can make my own decisions!'

'Son—'

'I'm not your son!'

Nathan gasped as Kieran continued his one-man show.

'"I think it'd be best if Kieran came to live with me, Mrs Ledley."' Kieran eyed the lamp on the side table.

'Kieran—,' Nathan said, trying to sound as calm as possible.

'I'm not your son! My dad's dead!' And with that, Kieran booted the lamp off the table, sending it crashing to the other side of the lounge.

'Kieran, your foot!' Nathan cried, almost diving on him.

'Get off me,' Kieran said, shrugging him off once more. He looked at Clarissa before limping across the lounge and up the stairs.

Was it you?' Kieran sat on the bed holding an ice pack to his foot.

Callum sat on the window ledge. 'Bruv, come on.' He flashed a lopsided smile at Kieran.

Kieran looked at his stepbrother and saw his rotting teeth and his new skinny frame that his borrowed clothes hung from.

'So that's it, is it?' Callum asked, running his hands through his messy brown hair. 'I'm an ex-con, so everything I say is a lie?' He then began to scratch his arms and neck.

Kieran sighed. 'I've let you into my home. I've trusted you.'

'And I'm thankful. What do you want me to do? Bow down to you?'

'Why?' Kieran asked, his eyes beginning to glaze over.

'It wasn't me,' Callum said. He continued to scratch himself and stare out of the bedroom window.

'You're lying.' A tear fell down Kieran's cheek. 'You haven't changed a bit.'

Callum turned to Kieran, tears now beginning to fill in his own eyes.

'Just like when we were kids,' Kieran continued. 'You kicked that stone into Mrs Quinn's car and broke her window.'

Callum wiped his tears furiously and continued to stare at his brother.

'You made us run, Callum. You made us swear it wasn't you, and you said that if I ever told anyone you'd break my legs.'

A silence fell over the room. Kieran winced and looked down at his swollen foot.

'I always looked after you,' Callum said as another tear streamed down his cheek. 'I was always the fall guy. You could never do any wrong.'

Kieran couldn't find a response.

'As soon as you came along, I was the bad apple.'

'Cal—'

'They all preferred you – Mum, Dad, Uncle Charlie.'

'Callum—'

The tears were flowing freely, roaming down his bony face. 'They tried to deny it, but it's always been the truth. And it ended up killing Dad.'

Kieran swallowed and blinked. He put a hand to his head and looked down.

'He was rushing to watch your game, golden boy. He would never rush to visit me.'

Kieran looked up. 'So this was revenge? That's why you sold the photos?'

'No,' Callum replied, wiping his face with his sleeve.

'Then, why?' Kieran asked, as another tear rolled down his cheek.

Callum didn't respond.

'Why?' Kieran asked once more.

Callum turned to his stepbrother. 'I had no choice. They said that they would hurt you, bruv. They're serious, these guys. I had to protect you, just like when we were at school.'

What are you talking about?' Kieran asked with a glower.

'They're gonna get me, then they're coming for you,' Callum went on.

'Who?'

Callum lowered his voice. 'Tiny,' he said.

Kieran looked on, confused. 'Tiny?'

'Yeah,' Callum replied. 'We were serving time together.'

Kieran was silent.

'He's still in there,' Callum continued. 'He runs a protection ring from inside.'

'How?' Kieran asked.

Callum shook his head. 'I don't know. He has a lot of people working for him. You hear things, and most of the time it's rumours. But Tiny's for real.'

Kieran attempted to stand up from the bed. 'Just hang on a second.' He winced and sat back down as soon as his swollen foot hit the ground. 'I don't understand. He's protecting you from inside?'

'No.' Callum looked Kieran dead in the eyes. 'He's protecting you, bruv. They know we're brothers and they're coming for you.'

'How do you know this guy's for real?'

'Because it's not just you. You're not the first. There's been others – football players, boxers.'

Kieran was perplexed. 'They target athletes then?'

Callum nodded slowly. 'And musicians … anyone they think needs protecting.'

'Protecting from what?!' Kieran shouted.

'From people like Tiny, who aren't on the inside.'

Kieran rubbed his face. He was confused. 'Look, Cal, I don't really get what the fuck is going on here. I think you're mixed up in some bad shit and you want money.'

'No!' Callum protested.

'You wanna buy some fucking drugs? Is that it?'

'No!' Callum shouted again. 'I'm clean. I didn't want to ask you for anything. That's why I sold the pictures.' Callum began to scratch himself again.

Kieran threw the ice pack on the ground, wetting the cream carpet.

'But I don't think it's enough, Kieran.'

'Not enough?' Kieran looked on, incredulous. 'You've given them money, and humiliated my fiancée in the process.'

'I'm sorry, bruv.' Callum went over and sat next to Kieran on the bed. 'I didn't know what else to do. Tiny's doing life for murder.'

'Jesus,' Kieran muttered. 'This is too much. I don't know how I ever thought this could work. You can't stay here anymore—'

'Where am I gonna go?'

'This isn't safe for Clarissa.' Kieran continued to speak right over Callum. 'It's not safe for me … who knows who's watching you? I don't know what you got up to, or who you pissed off when you were inside, but I can't have this shit in my life. I don't understand your world.'

Kieran paused, and both brothers stared out the bedroom window.

'They want ten per cent of your wages every week.'

It began to dawn on Kieran. 'The phone call at the restaurant.'

Callum didn't speak.

Kieran turned to him before shutting his eyes tightly. 'You can't stay here anymore.'

'Where am I going to go, Kieran?'

Nathan listened from the other side of the door. 'Fuck,' he said under his breath, before going back downstairs to pour a large drink.

DAILY REFLECTION

Saturday, 17th December, 2011

KIERAN LEDLEY DOESN'T PLAY

The Authenton forward will miss this afternoon's clash against Oldfield City after failing a fitness test on a swollen foot.

The star is said to have picked up the injury after stepping on some broken glass at a London nightclub last night. A fellow reveller said, 'Kieran and some mates took over the VIP section and were very merry, Kieran in particular. He seemed to be really enjoying himself, and at one stage he jumped up on his table and started dancing. It looked like he was only wearing socks on his feet, so that's when he must have hurt his foot.'

Authenton FC has refused to comment on these reports but the club manager, Alan Turble, will not be happy about this latest story about his star player. The 56-year-year-old Scotsman and 24-year-old Ledley are said to have a fractious relationship.

Earlier this month, as exclusively revealed by the *Daily Reflection*, naked pictures of the player's stunning fiancée, pop star Clarissa Harvey, surfaced.

The game kicks off at 3 p.m. today, Authenton sit three points clear at the top of the league.

CALLUM / RUPAL

When both Rupal's dealers didn't pick up she couldn't take it. She had sent them her usual text which read: *u around 2nite?* Normally Rupal would get a reply from at least one of them within five minutes. On the rare occasions her self-imposed time limit would pass, the frustration would begin. Rupal's body temperature would rise. She would attempt calming deep breaths while looking at her phone to make sure that her texts had been delivered. Then she would silently tell herself that she wasn't addicted to marijuana, that if she couldn't get hold of any tonight it would be fine, it wasn't the end of the world, and her world that was still happily spinning on its axis did not revolve around weed. At this point in her introspection approximately eight minutes would have passed since she had sent the text requests. And while continuing the muted conversation full of reassurances, she would simultaneously begin the countdown to ten minutes from the *message sent* time. Once that period had elapsed, Rupal would upgrade from texting and call the usually more reliable *W1* (W for weed). She would grind her teeth as the phone would ring and ring.

An increased heartbeat would come next as she attempted to convince herself that *W1* was in a loud place and therefore couldn't hear his phone. Hot, angry, and with an increasingly uncomfortable heartbeat, Rupal would now jump up from the sofa having just unsuccessfully attempted to phone her second, less reliable dealer, *W2*. 'Fucking dirty druggies,' she would moan. 'Probably getting high on their own supply.'

While throwing on an old pair of boots, Rupal would pretend that she wasn't affected by the irony of her last statement.

As she scraped her long black hair back into a ponytail and zipped up her grey hoody, Rupal would try to ignore the contradiction of the fact that she was about to head out and try to find some weed.

During Rupal's days in the force there was a running joke about an area not far from where George lived called Angetown. Such was the North London area's notoriety that whenever her colleagues were bored they would drive through Angetown and place bets on how many people were in the middle of a deal that very second. Little did Rupal know that notorious areas she became familiar with through work would become her saving grace. She had 'picked up' from random individuals there a couple of times. And here Rupal was again.

The run-down street still had the odd mattress or old vacuum dumped outside certain properties, but Rupal also noticed that most of the residents had made a good attempt at decorating the front of their houses with Christmas lights. She parked her car and walked round the corner looking for the alley she was familiar with.

She squinted into the darkness and could make out a skinny figure. Putting up her hood and doing her best to not appear like an intimidated former copper, Rupal approached the skinny man and nodded at him before saying, 'You got anything, mate?'

The man waved a dismissive hand towards her. 'Nah, nah.'

'Just weed, mate?' Rupal heard her voice in her head and couldn't tell what accent she had just attempted.

He looked around again nervously before shaking his head and saying, 'Nah.'

Rupal also took a quick glance out into the darkness. 'Mate—'

'Fuck off, alright?' the man interrupted.

The words seemed to send a jolt through Rupal, for she immediately turned around and headed out of the alley.

'Jesus Christ,' she whispered to herself.

As she emerged from the blackness Rupal couldn't decide if she felt more scared or humiliated. Just then a young male walked past. He was wearing a rucksack and he looked like a student. Rupal watched the chubby white kid. Their eyes met briefly, and even though Rupal thought that he didn't look like a typical drug dealer, she reminded herself of the countless surprises she had encountered during her time as a policewoman. *And besides*, she told herself, *he's probably a student. Which student doesn't smoke weed?*

Rupal caught up with the chubby young man. 'You got anything, mate?'

The student-type slowed down and glanced sideways at Rupal. 'Do I know you?'

'I'm not from this area,' Rupal replied, once again adopting a strange accent.

The chubby young man looked around the dark street. 'What you after?'

'Just a bit of green?' said Rupal, feigning nonchalance.

'Weed, yeah?'

'Err … yeah,' Rupal replied, fearing whether her use of the term 'green' had given her away. She began to wonder whether it was an outdated piece of slang, or whether her fake accent had sounded silly. *Shit*, she thought. *I'm so obvious. All I want is a bit of—*

The chubby young man hooked his thumbs through his rucksack straps. He looked Rupal up and down and smiled. 'Are you a fed?'

'What?' Rupal replied, hoping that her high-pitched response would be perceived as genuine shock by the student.

'You the police?'

Rupal shook her head and suddenly felt a bit dizzy.

'Okay, how much you want?'

'Err …' Rupal was becoming a bona fide pothead but she still wasn't sure of the measurements. 'Twenty … pounds worth?'

The chubby young man played with his top lip. 'Twos, yeah?'

Rupal nodded. 'Yes … yeah.'

'Cool.' The chubby young man looked around once more before reaching into his pocket. They did the deal and Rupal couldn't be sure but she thought that he attempted to hold onto her hand as she drew it away.

Rupal quickly walked away from the chubby young man who called, 'Don't you wanna save my number?'

Rupal didn't respond, instead hotfooting it back to her car. She walked past the alley and quickly peered into the darkness where she could still make out the shape of the skinny man that had told her to fuck off. He appeared to be talking to another figure.

Callum shook hands with the hooded man, the transaction expertly carried out but for his slight tremble. It was the first time Callum had scored since he was released, and he was excited. He really did want to be clean, he really did wish to start again, but he was stressed. Callum pocketed the crack, paid for by some of the money Clarissa's nude photos had raised.

Crouched at the entrance of the dark alley, Rupal was still watching. *You can take the girl out of the force ...* Before she could complete the saying in her head, Rupal could see that the skinny man was now headed in her direction. She quickly darted round the corner and continued to hide.

Exiting the dark alley Callum told himself that this was just a blip. He may have just bought some crack but *he* hadn't cracked. He just needed something to alleviate the increased pressure moving back in with his mum had caused. A woman who, despite still trying to love him as much as she could, struggled to conceal her disappointment in him. Callum needed something to relieve the anxiety that dumping a bag full of more money than he had ever seen in a park had brought about. And he needed something to numb the headache he felt as he tried to work out how he could get his stepbrother to part with twenty thousand pounds a week. Callum avoided a puddle as a black car screeched to a halt in front of him. He looked up and was blinded by the vehicle's headlights. Condensation escaped from his mouth into the cold air.

Rupal continued to spy as the skinny man took a step back and fell into the puddle behind him. Two figures emerged from the bright light and yanked him to his feet. He made a futile attempt to wriggle free from their vice-like grip but the men were too strong. They bundled him into the back of the car. Rupal instinctively reached for her radio on her shoulder – except it wasn't there. She looked down at her clothes – her hoody, her old pair of ill-fitting jeans and even older boots. She remembered that she no longer worked for the law. 'Shit,' she whispered as her heart raced even further. Rupal reached into her back pocket and brought out her mobile phone. Her thumb hovered over the number nine and she sighed. She reached into another pocket and brought out the bag of weed. Looking at both items in each of her hands, Rupal shook her head. 'Fuck.' She ran towards her car and decided to get the hell out of Angetown.

'Callum,' the gentle voice came from a medium-built man who sat beside Callum at the back. 'Tiny is working on his patience. But you're not making it easy for him.'

Callum squinted, trying to see past the purple dots cavorting in front of his eyes. He couldn't make out the face of the person speaking to him.

'Now,' the gentle voice continued, 'we know you're staying with your mother. So we know where to find her, no problem. But what you're going to do now is give us your black brother's address.'

When Callum opened his mouth to speak, the man brought a pistol out of his jacket and placed it between Callum's lips.

'If the first words that come out of your mouth aren't Kieran Ledley's address, I'm going to make you swallow my gun's cum.'

KIERAN, 2012

The tyres crackled over the pebbles in the drive as the animalistic roar of the engine began to fade. Kieran pushed the button, switching off the engine of his new white Lamborghini. Who cares if he already had one? This one was a different colour to his yellow model. This was a present to himself, bought with his goal scoring bonus, a little something to celebrate his team reaching the final of the FA Cup. Career-wise, things couldn't be going more swimmingly for Kieran Ledley. On the pitch he was living up to his price tag, 'If there's any player worth 70 million, it's Ledley', according to the back page of one newspaper. 'KIERAN LED-GEND!' praised another. But off the pitch there was nothing to celebrate. His real life was empty. A beautiful fiancée whom he never saw, a 'National Treasure' in the making who was merely his arm candy. The times when they were snapped as a couple on red carpets were often the only times they were together.

The gates to his mansion slowly closed behind him and Kieran exited his low vehicle and approached his front door. He normally looked forward to being swallowed by his home. It had once been the only sanctuary inside his goldfish bowl of an existence, the one place he felt safe.

This was all before Callum had come back into his life. Kieran liked to think that he wasn't a paranoid person; he tried to avoid always travelling with the bodyguard assigned to him by his club. When Authenton's new Middle Eastern owner's assured him that they had to 'make sure our most valuable asset is adequately protected', he couldn't help feeling like a piece of meat. But he now knew that he couldn't ignore the anonymous calls he had received over the past few months. Who, Kieran wondered, was the man in Vivian's car park? He couldn't shake off the shadow of paranoia that Callum had introduced into his life. Even though Kieran had evicted his stepbrother and unceremoniously ended their reunion, he'd had no choice but to up the security at his home.

Kieran frowned as he wondered why his front door was ajar. Clarissa wasn't due back from an overseas engagement for another two days. Perhaps Nathan, the only other person with the security code, had forgotten to close the door behind him? Knowing this was unlikely, as Nathan was never careless when it came to safety, Kieran slowly backed away and reached for his phone.

The first person he thought to call was his agent. The phone rang through his handset, and after a beat, Kieran could hear a ringing coming from inside his house. Without hesitation Kieran entered his property.

His white marble floor was covered in shattered glass from the now empty trophy cabinet in the corner. There were two sets of large muddy footprints on the stairs ahead of him.

'Nathan …?' Kieran called out in fear, his voice echoing through the large foyer. He heard the last of the phone's rings and followed the sound to the landing around the corner.

Nathan was lying there, the left side of his face swollen, his grey blazer tossed aside, his white shirt ripped open and covered in blood, his trembling hand attempting to grip his mobile phone.

'It's not as bad as it looks,' he said, involuntarily squinting through his newly bruised eyes.

Kieran rushed over to him. 'What the fuck happened?'

'It was just a warning. It'll all be sorted soon.'

'I'm calling the police,' Kieran said, putting his phone to his ear.

'No, don't!' Nathan shouted.

Kieran looked at the pathetic fat mess on the floor.

'Please don't,' Nathan said, managing to rise to his knees. 'They'll be straight on to the press. It'll all be fucked.'

'Shit!' Kieran shouted. He ran back over to his front door and slammed it before violently punching in the security code. Kieran rounded the corner again and helped his agent to his feet. 'Did you manage to get a look at them?'

'They're not going away,' Nathan said, no longer attempting to reassure Kieran.

'I'm so sorry, Nathan.' Kieran picked his agent's blazer up from the floor and handed it to him. 'Callum has got me into some shit. I've been receiving threatening calls. The first one was towards the end of last year ...'

Nathan placed his blazer on the sofa and looked into his client's eyes. 'I know.'

Kieran tilted his head to one side, confused.

'I heard you guys talking. I was listening from outside the room. I know everything.'

Kieran went over to the kitchen and returned with a glass of whisky for Nathan. 'What are we going to do?'

Nathan downed the drink and shrugged. 'They said that unless twenty thousand pounds is deposited into this account ...' Nathan fished a scrunched up piece of paper out of his back pocket and placed it on the coffee table, it had some numbers written on it, 'by midday tomorrow, and every Friday after that, they're going to make sure that you're dead before the FA Cup Final.'

The two of them flopped down onto the L-shaped sofa and sat in silence for a few minutes, looking around the overturned lounge.

Nathan topped up his glass before saying, 'I also have a gambling problem, and I'm seven hundred and fifty thousand pounds in debt.'

Kieran watched Nathan down another shot of whisky. 'We're in too deep now, son.'

KIERAN, TUESDAY 3 P.M.

'I urge you to go to the police, Kieran.' Vivian's experience was being tested to the limit. She was doing everything she could to maintain her composure. 'You have received numerous threatening phone calls, you are being held to ransom, your home was broken into, and your agent was attacked.' She watched her patient hold eye contact with her for longer than normal. Vivian felt Kieran was studying her for the first time. Even though they had now shared many sessions together, Vivian was certain that Kieran was more familiar with her voice than her appearance. She would observe him train his eyes over the carpet as she spoke to him, her voice consistently calm. But today Vivian noticed that Kieran had been looking at her as she attempted to convey the danger that Callum had brought into his life since his release. Vivian hoped that despite how unruffled she was trying to sound, Kieran could see the concern in her eyes. 'This is an incredibly serious situation.' Vivian clasped her hands in front of her.

Kieran took a deep breath and exhaled slowly. 'I can't go to the police.'

'Kieran, listen to me. I am not going to let anything happen to another one of my patients.' She took in the change in Kieran's facial expression and she suspected he was now demonstrating slight confusion at her last statement. She blinked a few times in an attempt to flush the images of Gemma and Pete that were starting to tiptoe through her mind. Vivian collected herself, and after a beat she continued, 'You are putting me in a very difficult position.'

'Whoa,' Kieran said, raising his hand, 'Nathan told me that these sessions were confidential. I thought I could trust you.'

'Kieran—' Vivian attempted to interrupt.

'No,' Kieran continued, not letting her. 'What about patient confidentiality?'

'Your life is in danger. This is beyond that.' Vivian was about to speak again but she caught herself.

She thought about her ex-husband and the years of abuse he'd subjected her to. She remembered how long she'd endured her hell before eventually reporting him. 'I know this is difficult. I understand.'

'I don't think you do.'

Their eyes remained locked. 'Trust me, I do. You feel trapped, as if there is nobody you can turn to. You feel as if you will be judged.' Vivian could see that she now had Kieran's undivided attention. 'You can already hear people saying that you brought it upon yourself. You feel alone, and scared.'

Kieran nodded slowly.

Vivian leaned forward. 'Please, go to the police.'

Kieran put his hands to his face, momentarily breaking their eye contact. He sank back into the sofa before revealing his tears. Vivian went over to her side table and grabbed a bunch of tissues. She sat back down and offered them to Kieran. He took them from her, wiped his face then said, 'The press would go crazy if this got out—'

'Forget the press,' Vivian appealed. 'How much money are you going to keep paying these people? For how long? People like them count on fear. Enough is enough, Kieran. You don't deserve this.'

Kieran stared at Vivian.

'These people count on fear.' Vivian repeated. 'This is extortion, and as long as you continue to pay them they are getting what they want. I don't believe they intend to kill you.'

Kieran remained silent.

'What are they to gain from doing so?' Vivian took in the sight of her frightened patient. *Fifth Wall,* she told herself. 'These crooks have seen their opportunity and want it to last. Killing you wouldn't benefit them.'

'These people are more than crooks, Vivian.' said Kieran. 'They are in prison for life. They've killed people before. They have nothing to lose.'

Vivian leaned forward. 'Which is why I am begging you to go to the police … or at least talk to someone at the club. The chairman, your manager … somebody.' Vivian could hear the desperation returning to her voice. She breathed slowly and took in the sight of Kieran shaking his head and no longer wiping his tears.

Vivian spoke again. 'Just because I don't think they will follow through with their threats, it doesn't mean you should remain silent.' Vivian watched her patient staring back at her, expressionless. As the ghosts of Gemma and Pete floated past, she could only hope that her words were getting through to Kieran.

RUPAL

It was the third call she had received from George but once again Rupal diverted it. She threw her mobile on the back seat. Rupal and George had been arguing quite a lot lately. A little more than a new couple should. And deep down Rupal knew she was mostly to blame. At first it was George who mentioned his insecurities about his girlfriend having a more 'grown-up' profession than his retail job. Rupal would reassure him by saying that 'some people take a little longer to find their way.'

She would also tell him that it was nice that they both worked shifts which allowed them to lie in together from time to time. But ever since Rupal had quit her job the mood of their relationship had changed. She hated seeing George go off to work, and then him coming back hours later to find her on the sofa, or still in the same clothes as when he'd left. This was not her at all. She always prided herself on earning a living, on being independent – not a little Indian girl whose parents had her future mapped out. But at the moment, Rupal herself didn't know what the future had in store for her. She would lounge around all day, watching rubbish daytime TV, waiting for George to come home. Once he'd arrived via the local Chinese takeaway, they would eat in front of the television while he shared amusing anecdotes about customers. Just when Rupal would be getting bored of these tales, they would roll up a joint, smoke until they could barely keep their eyes open, and then, if they had the energy, have rushed sex.

Soon, Rupal would start smoking in the afternoon, and these sessions became earlier and more frequent, eventually leading to her smoking throughout the day. And it was when George told her that she needed to take it easy, and that it wasn't nice for him to come home to a girlfriend who was half-asleep at six o'clock in the evening, and to a flat that reeked of marijuana, that they had their first blazing row.

After this, Rupal endeavoured to not be at the flat when George got home from work. And she made sure she took her weed with her.

Rupal put the joint to her lips and took a long, slow drag. She wound the window down, leaving a small gap. Reclining in her seat, she allowed the cannabis to take hold and relax her. Rupal exhaled a neat puff of smoke through her nostrils and told herself to stop feeling guilty about the night when she'd run away from what had looked like some sort of kidnapping. For all she knew it had been just a little dispute. Nobody got hurt. And besides, she didn't work for the police anymore, she'd contributed more than enough to the justice system, and – she was now starting to become agitated at the thoughts interrupting her high – *what fucking support have they given me since I left?*

Raindrops began to fall and Rupal could hear every single one land on her windscreen. Her eyes darted as she tried to count the drops in her head. She giggled as her calculations veered off track, and then watched the drops trickle down. She placed an imaginary bet on a particular larger drop and quietly cheered when it won its race down the windscreen.

Rupal sucked on her spliff continuously as a black cat tentatively made its way out of an alley. It hopped onto a bin opposite the car, and Rupal engaged in a staring contest with it. Its pretty eyes appeared to glow in the dark and the cat and Rupal gaped at each other for what seemed like forever. Rupal decided that the cat was female.

'That's it girl, feisty. Stand up for yourself.' Giggling at her commentary, Rupal called after the cat as it darted away. 'No, come back. Hey, feisty, where are you going?'

Rupal puffed again and held the joint between her lips – which were now a little bit burnt – as she ran both hands through her thick black hair. An upstairs light came on in a house across the road. Paranoid, Rupal peered up at the twitching curtains. She squinted towards the lit room before muttering, 'Fuck you, what have you done for justice?'

Rupal looked in her rear-view mirror and saw a flickering white light. Thinking it was a small fairy, she smiled and continued to smoke. The light got bigger and came closer, and Rupal simply stared. The light was followed by the faint sound of a bicycle chain and Rupal could now see that it was somebody riding a bike. The light slowly morphed into a yellow reflective jacket and the rider seemed to glide past in slow motion before casting a quick glance towards Rupal's car. It looked as though the cyclist was riding off into the night, but at the last minute they rode in a short circle before heading back towards her car. Rupal recognised the stance of the police cyclist reaching over to their shoulder and speaking into a radio.

'Shit.' Rupal leaned over to the passenger door and rolled down the window before throwing what was left of her joint out of it.

Just then, the police cyclist knocked on her window.

The face was obscured by the shadow cast by the helmet but Rupal could tell it was a male.

'Shit,' Rupal said again as she settled back into her seat.

'Wind the window down please,' the male voice said.

Rupal looked down towards her thighs and let out a deep sigh before following the instruction.

'What are you doing sat here this evening, madam?' the policeman asked, still straddling his bicycle.

Rupal continued to look down. 'Nothing.'

'Nothing?' the policeman replied. 'So that isn't cannabis I can smell coming from your car?'

Rupal didn't respond.

'Waiting for someone are you?' the policeman asked.

Silence.

'Right,' the policeman said, resting his bicycle against a hedge. 'Can you step out of the car, please?'

Rupal remained still and silent, trying to bring her racing heartbeat under control.

'Madam?' the policeman said, crouching towards the window. 'Let's not make this difficult.'

When Rupal looked up they both held their mouths open but couldn't speak.

The policeman squinted into the dark car, and after a beat said, 'Rupal? Is that you?'

Thinking she was hallucinating, Rupal's now saucer-like eyes widened. 'Nikesh?'

The policeman removed his cycling helmet: black hair, light-brown skin – Rupal could see that it was indeed her former colleague.

'Rupal? What the fuck?' He let out a faint chuckle before walking round to the passenger side of the car. Rupal heard him say 'false alarm' into his radio, before getting in.

Rupal put her head in her hands, and they sat in silence for a while until Nikesh said, 'So … is this what you've been spending your time doing?'

Rupal's shoulders were heaving, and after a few moments she looked up and said, 'Fuck you,' with a giggle. They both laughed and Rupal shook her head. 'I was absolutely shitting myself!'

'What are you doing smoking in the street?' Nikesh asked.

Rupal pinched the bridge of her nose with her thumb and forefinger. 'I just needed to get out of the house.'

Nikesh spoke softly, 'What about if it had been a different copper going past?'

'Whatever,' Rupal replied. 'I don't care.'

'I thought you said you were shitting yourself.'

'Don't start with me, Nikesh. Don't fucking judge me.'

'I'm not,' Nikesh replied defensively. 'I'm just saying you could have got yourself into trouble.'

'I'm a big girl. I can look after myself.'

They sat in silence and both watched the raindrops dancing across the windscreen.

A car drove past and Nikesh turned to Rupal. 'I've texted you a few times and you've never replied. I've been a bit worried.'

Rupal shook her head.

'I have,' said Nikesh. 'I'm not the only one, Kerry's been asking about you too.'

'Ah, Kerry,' Rupal reminisced with sarcastic fondness. 'The bike of the team.'

'Hey!' Nikesh replied in a prickly tone. 'We've just started seeing each other—'

'Oh God ...' Rupal interrupted.

'Maybe I should arrest you after all!' Nikesh continued.

Rupal folded her arms and chuckled to herself.

Nikesh watched her. 'Are the rumours about Kerry true, then?'

Rupal lay back in her seat and gave an indifferent shrug.

They sat in silence until Nikesh said, 'Seriously, Rupal, how have you been? One minute you were around, and the next you just disappeared. Are you okay?'

'No I'm not bloody okay,' Rupal slurred. 'What's all this fake concern? You should have been there when it mattered.'

Nikesh scratched his head and sighed. 'You're not still upset about the incident at the pub are you?'

Rupal's eyes became even wider. 'Oh, so you now acknowledge it was an incident? I thought it was "no big deal".'

Nikesh sighed again. 'So they used the "Paki" word—'

'Bandied it about casually, more like.' Rupal interrupted.

'So what?'

Rupal was astounded. 'So what?'

'Yeah, so what?' Nikesh said again. 'If I was to confront everyone who said that or anything else inappropriate, I'd need to smoke weed on duty to calm down.'

After her former colleague's comment, there was a brief halt to their exchange and Rupal laughed.

Nikesh joined in. 'Come on,' he said, 'you know it's true.'

'It's not just that,' said Rupal. 'It's the sexism too.'

'Yes,' Nikesh agreed. 'And the lack of appreciation by some members of the public for what we do. The relentless hours, the rubbish pay, the danger, all of it. But ultimately we do it to make a difference. And I think we do make a difference.'

Rupal frowned, looked out the window, then turned back to Nikesh.

'What?' Nikesh asked.

'Humph,' was all Rupal said.

Nikesh grinned. 'When did I become so smart, right?

Rupal smiled. 'Shut up.'

'Come on!' Nikesh said, his grin becoming wider. 'Everyone knows Indians are the smartest!'

'Correction,' Rupal replied. 'Everyone knows Indian women are the smartest!'

Nikesh held his hands up and they both laughed.

'I'm so fucking high.'

'Come on Roops,' said Nikesh. 'Let's switch seats, I'll lock up my bike and drive you home.' Nikesh exited the car and secured his bicycle against a railing.

He walked over to the driver's seat and Rupal allowed herself to be guided out from behind the wheel and around the car to the passenger side.

Within minutes they had arrived at George's flat. Nikesh walked Rupal to the front door of the converted building where they were met by Rupal's annoyed but worried-looking boyfriend. He ran a hand over his short brown hair and tutted as he stood there barefoot in an oversized green T-shirt and pyjama bottoms. 'I've been trying to call you.' He held out his arms and Rupal embraced him.

'Goodnight guys.' Nikesh offered Rupal's car keys to George who noticed him for the first time.

George furrowed his brows as he took in Nikesh's uniform, and he watched Nikesh walk off. 'Come on,' he said, looking down at his girlfriend. 'Let's get you inside.'

KIERAN, 2012

Kieran danced down the right wing, evading the outstretched leg of United's left back. On reaching the by-line he dragged the ball back with his right foot, sending Jones the wrong way. Oblivious of the red laser dot on his forehead, Kieran looked up and saw his teammate, Darren Sands, running into the penalty box waving his hands frantically, screaming for the delivery. With an effortless swing of his left foot, Kieran obliged. Darren's forehead connected with the ball, sending it crashing into the back of the net. Authenton were one–nil up in the FA Cup Final. Kieran turned to one corner of the crowd and Wembley Stadium erupted. The sound was so deafening that it seemed every person in the stands was an Authenton FC fan. Kieran looked at the euphoric blur in front of him.

He wished he could feel like this forever, as if he were floating on a cloud of ecstasy, a cloud so big that he felt incredibly safe.

Everything seemed to be moving in slow motion as the sea of people jumped up and down and swayed from side to side. Kieran mattered; to these people he was a hero, a king. Not a little brown boy with white parents. Not a skinny little kid nursing a black eye from a familiar beating.

Kieran's triumphant thoughts were buried as his teammates piled on top of him. Emerging from the celebration, Kieran jogged back to the halfway line. The red dot was now on his chest. Simultaneous flashes emitted from the stands but one stood out as the brightest. Bang. Down Kieran went in the centre of the field, clutching his chest.

Kieran sat up in the bed. He felt his exposed chest and looked down. He ran a hand across his sweaty forehead and saw his teammate, Darren, sleeping in the bed on the other side of the room. Kieran looked at the digital clock on the table beside him. It was three twenty in the morning, less than twelve hours until kick-off. Kieran couldn't see how he could play in the game; he had to get out of the hotel.

RUPAL, MONDAY 11 A.M.

'George was so understanding. It made me realise how much I've taken him for granted.'

Vivian smiled and nodded at Rupal. 'It's easily done.'

Rupal was sat cross-legged on the sofa. She fiddled with her ponytail while looking at the carpet, before exhaling and meeting Vivian's eyes.

'Your hair looks nice.'

'Oh,' Vivian replied, slightly embarrassed. She gently touched her short trim. 'I just took a little more off the sides and dyed the top a darker brown.'

'Suits you,' said Rupal.

'Thanks. I fancied a change … So' – Vivian flicked through her notes – 'you haven't smoked for three weeks?'

Rupal groaned dramatically. 'Yeah. It's been bloody hard.'

'Congratulations,' Vivian replied. 'I know it's not easy.'

Rupal nodded and puffed her cheeks. 'Oh, and I've got back in touch with a couple of the guys from work.'

Vivian jotted something down and then looked up at Rupal. 'It's interesting that you still refer to your old job as work.'

'What do you mean?' Rupal asked, curling her lips downwards.

'Well,' Vivian said, adjusting her smart, dark-green jumper dress. 'It's quite a while since you worked there, and you still refer to it as such.'

Rupal looked at the wall behind Vivian and thought for a moment. 'I guess …

it's because it was a huge part of my life.'

Vivian poured some water for Rupal and flicked through her file once more. 'Tell me a little bit more about your somewhat fortunate reunion with "Politically Correct" Nikesh.'

Rupal put her face in her hands and laughed. 'Argghh. It was awful!'

Vivian joined in the laughter. 'It seems to have turned out to be a good thing.'

Rupal rested her head back on the sofa and looked up at the ceiling. 'It's been quite nice to know people have asked about me at work … I mean, at the force.'

Vivian smiled, acknowledging Rupal's slip of the tongue.

'But it also made me realise that I don't actually miss the job. And after that night Nikesh caught me, I realised that sitting around hasn't been healthy for me.' She drank from her glass. 'I've started to get out of the house more. It's amazing how stepping out for an hour or two can really invigorate you …' Rupal paused. 'I know it sounds quite pathetic.'

'Not at all,' said Vivian.

A blush glowed on each of Rupal's light-brown cheeks. 'Okay, but I think you might laugh at this next bit. I've been making lists – things I need to get done on each day—'

'What's wrong with that?' Vivian asked softly.

'No, some of the tasks are the most mundane things. I'm talking take out the trash, buy a new mop, remind George to renew his resident's parking permit!'

Vivian laughed.

'You see!' Rupal cringed. 'I knew you'd laugh!'

Vivian held up both hands, revealing her freshly manicured nails. 'I'm laughing at the familiarity of it all! You wanna see my to-do list! It's absolutely ridiculous!'

Both women giggled.

'You like structure,' Vivian continued, 'and that can become magnified when you go from being busy, to not being busy.'

Rupal reflected on that and nodded. 'It's actually been quite helpful in taking my mind off smoking …' Rupal blushed again. 'Every little helps. And talking of structure, George and I have been trying to do different things in the evenings. Eating out, or I meet him in town after work.'

'That's great.' Vivian replied.

'We were having coffee the other day, and I was rambling on as I usually do—'

Vivian smiled cheekily, 'You? Never.'

Rupal smiled back and rolled her eyes, 'Whatever! Anyway, I was nattering away and George said, "You know what, babe? I think you should consider becoming a motivational speaker!" I thought he was taking the piss but he said he wasn't, and I've been thinking about it quite a lot ever since.'

Vivian tilted her head and watched Rupal's eyes widen excitedly.

'I think I want to become a motivational speaker for women.'

As Rupal continued to ramble on, Vivian smiled.

DAILY REFLECTION

Saturday, 5th May, 2012

KIERAN LEDLEY AWOL

Today Authenton fans should be celebrating. They are about to play in their first FA Cup Final in seven years, and could be about to end their season with a remarkable league and cup double. The league champions arrived at their hotel last night but had a notable absentee.

The player in question is none other than star Kieran Ledley. The 24-year-old forward has had a successful first season with Authenton, scoring 38 goals in all appearances since his record £70 million move from Albans Town. He helped lead his team to their first league championship in 6 years, and his 4 goals and 7 assists in the FA Cup have been instrumental in leading the club to the final of the competition.

With the champions having qualified for the lucrative Champions League for the second successive season since being reintroduced to the competition last year for the first time since 2006, many believe that Ledley has already repaid his incredible transfer fee.

But his first season with Authenton hasn't been without controversy. As much as he graces the back pages for his sporting achievements, Kieran Ledley is also often front page news.

Famous for his long-term relationship with 24-year-old pop star Clarissa Harvey, Ledley has also been the subject of numerous 'kiss and tells' over the last few years.

During a recent post-match interview, he was questioned about the headlines on that morning's front pages claiming that he had been 'boozing it up at a nightclub until 3 a.m.' He responded by saying that the press liked to paint him as a bad boy, and that he was targeted because he was with a famous singer. There were rumours that Authenton FC's owners, the Karim brothers, overruled head coach Alan Turble when he tried to drop Ledley for a game. Incident's like these have led to many stories about dressing room bust-ups this season, with Ledley's teammates disgruntled about the apparent favouritism towards their star player.

The club's successful season was also threatened to be derailed by a fallout amongst the back-room staff after a statement Turble made following the team's shock home defeat to Stavely. During the game, owners Imran and Adeel Karim, 39 and 42 years old respectively, allegedly told the manager that he couldn't substitute Kieran Ledley.

When asked about this after the match, Turble simply said, 'Things were a lot easier when we were a so-called "small club", and I was allowed to be a manager.'

Alan Turble later issued a statement saying that he regretted the remark and that he had said it in anger after the loss.

Despite this, the 56-year-old has won many new fans this year with neutrals impressed by the dignified manner in which he has conducted himself over what has ultimately been a successful season.

But this latest story once again threatens to overshadow what could be a glorious end to Authenton's campaign. Countless rumours have emerged over the last few hours as to Ledley's whereabouts, with some people suggesting that he has refused to travel with the team after a training ground bust-up with club captain, Darren Sands. There have been reports of 'sightings', with one woman claiming to have seen him in party capital Ibiza in the last 24 hours. One Internet blog has suggested that the player has 'escaped to Las Vegas to marry Clarissa Harvey.'

The most shocking and somewhat disturbing Chinese whisper is that the player has been kidnapped.

Kieran's stepbrother, Callum, was released from prison late last year after serving two and a half years for armed robbery.

They were photographed together at their father's funeral last year, and ever since, Kieran has been dogged by rumours that he has been targeted by drug dealers that his stepbrother was allegedly involved with while serving time.

A source close to club said, 'Truth be told, nobody actually knows where Kieran is. The team was given some time off after the season, but they all reported back for training last week in preparation for the final, including Kieran.' The source added, 'He seemed to be in good spirits and was joking with the rest of the lads.'

The club has declined to comment, and Ledley's agent, Nathan Rougel, could not be reached.

The game kicks off at 3 p.m. this afternoon. Whether Kieran Ledley, the world's most expensive player, will be on Authenton's team sheet remains to be seen.

KIERAN, 2012

Kieran lay back and listened to the subtle hum of the air con as the two girls performed oral sex on him. He looked down and saw the pale girl's head bobbing up and down, her short black hair harsh against her skin. The other girl flicked her red hair behind her ear and rubbed Kieran's chest, then she curled her lipstick-stained mouth into a fiendish smile before crawling up his body and kissing him.

Closing his eyes, Kieran was doing everything he could to get lost, to escape, to match the feeling of scoring a match-winning goal.

Despite being knee deep in alcohol and skin deep in the Russian prostitutes, Kieran couldn't drown out the truth. There was nowhere for the star to hide. How long could he hibernate in a London hotel room before his absence became big news?

He could drink until he burst, and he could fuck every whore the concierge sent his way, but it wouldn't change the fact that he was on the run. It wouldn't change the fact that he had deserted his team on the eve of their most important game, and that he had stopped paying the so-called 'protection money'.

Kieran let out a stifled growl when he ejaculated. The Russians fell by his side as he pondered how his momentary eruption of pleasure hadn't altered the fact that he felt he was on borrowed time.

The one with the dark hair threw a look back to Kieran as she made her way to the bathroom. Kieran watched her perfect form disappear. He wondered how Clarissa was feeling. He considered how many messages would be waiting for him when he eventually switched his phone on. How panicked would Nathan be? How irate would Alan Turble be? What would the reaction be at his failure to show up for the big game? He didn't know how the situation could ever be remedied.

He reached down to the floor in search of the bottle of vodka. When he couldn't find it he rubbed his face and tapped the redhead beside him. 'Babe,' he said, trying to ignore his sore throat, 'pass me the bottle, please.'

As the redhead reached down, the door burst open. Four masked gunmen swiftly entered the room, with one of them opening fire from a silenced pistol. Before the redhead could utter a word, she was hit by a bullet.

Kieran looked down at her slumped body and saw the hole between her eyes. Blood streamed from her head, as if her red hair was leaking. There was silence as he slipped on the claret soaked bed sheets. Another of the gunmen fired another silent shot as Kieran dived off the bed.

He lay on the ground, staring up at the ceiling, and realised there was no more time for him left to borrow.

The four masked gunmen walked round the bed and concurrently fired their silent pistols into Kieran's body. They watched his eyes fall open, and saw the blood stream from his mouth.

One of the gunmen put a gloved hand to Kieran's throat and felt for a pulse. 'He's dead.' The other three nodded and walked back round the bed, stepping over the lifeless prostitute's body, and out of the suite.

The dark-haired girl peered round the bathroom door. She was trembling, her mascara was smudged, and a black tear streamed down her cheek as she saw feathers falling from the ceiling. She looked at Kieran's bullet-riddled body before taking in the twisted, bloody mess of her colleague. As the dark-haired prostitute moved her mouth to speak, she stumbled forward and vomited.

NATHAN

Nathan was still driving. He didn't know where he was going but as he was speeding along the motorway the montage continued. He couldn't get the image of Kieran's lifeless body out of his head. His fleshy cheeks stung from the dry tears left over from when he held the frail Anna Ledley as she attempted to throw herself to the ground when the coroner revealed her son's corpse.

Nathan had clenched his jaw so hard that his teeth had begun to hurt. *No, no, no.* His cerebral dialogue went, as he held a shaking Anna. *It's not him. It can't be. It's not my son under there.*

The coroner had lifted the white sheet. Nathan tried to hold on to Anna as she fell, all the while keeping his eyes trained on the inanimate Kieran. He took in the single bullet hole to the head. He saw the entry points on the torso. Nathan blinked continuously and Kieran's peaceful-looking face slowly morphed into that of his eight-year-old son.

After dropping Anna at her brother's house, Nathan started the engine of his Range Rover, but he didn't know where he was going. All he knew was that he hadn't saved Kieran. Just like he hadn't saved his son seventeen years ago. He gripped the steering wheel as he jostled with the guilt of letting Anna down, and he began to cry again as he wished he had done more to prevent Callum from re-entering Kieran's life. He thought about Clarissa. Kieran had only been dead a few hours but he knew it wouldn't be long before the world was aware of it. The last thing he wanted was for his client's fiancée to hear about it on the news. Nathan had done everything he could to contact Clarissa on his way to the morgue. He had even resorted to sending her private messages via social media, but the Atlantic Ocean and a different time zone had made it difficult to reach her.

Nathan was on autopilot. He put his foot through the accelerator and his mind continued to overflow with thoughts. He was struggling to fathom the impact that Kieran's death would make.

The car groaned as Nathan put all his considerable weight on the pedal, swallowing the empty road in front of him. As the vehicle powered its way through the dark, he began to recognise the route.

Without thinking, he had embarked on a journey he had made almost seventeen years ago. He was driving to Beachy Head. Nathan didn't slow down as he neared his destination. He was determined that this would be different from his previous visit. In 1995, after standing on the edge of the cliff, he eventually decided that he had something to live for. Now he wasn't so sure. His marriage had long failed, and as far as he was concerned tonight's tragedy had confirmed his failure as a father for the second time.

Nathan's nails dug into his palms. He was squeezing the life out of the steering wheel in the same way he wanted to squeeze the life out of himself. He ruminated on the nature of his existence: an overweight man nearing fifty. A man who had once thought that his pursuit of happiness had ended when his 'second son' had turned professional. He was certain that all his troubles would be solved once he had guided Kieran to his millions.

Nathan exited the motorway and in an instant his despair turned into anger. What was the point of it all? he asked himself. The richer Kieran became, the more in debt he himself became. He reflected on the night when Kieran's house had been broken into by gangsters. He asked himself if things would have been different if they had gone to the police.

He looked back over his countless encounters with prostitutes – women with problems of their own whom he knew were disgusted by the sight of his fat old body. He thought about how Kieran had inherited his dependency on vice girls.

Looking out into the darkness, and telling himself that he was as much to blame for both of his sons' deaths as anybody else, Nathan accelerated towards the edge of the cliff and sent himself and his car into a free fall that mirrored his life.

DAILY REFLECTION

Monday, 7th May, 2012

KIERAN LEDLEY FOUND DEAD

The body of the world's most expensive football player, Kieran Ledley, was found in the King Suite of Hyde Park's Summit Hotel in the early hours of this morning. He had nine bullet holes in his torso and was pronounced dead at the scene.

The body of an unidentified young woman was also found at the bloody scene. The woman, thought to be in her early twenties, had a single bullet wound in her head.

A female witness – whose identity cannot be revealed – says that she was in the bathroom of the hotel suite when she heard a commotion. Fearing for her safety, she remained there until she heard a voice say, 'He's dead.' When she emerged from hiding, she found the body of the English football player and the young woman.

Two ambulance crews arrived at the hotel within five minutes of receiving the call, according to a spokeswoman.

Chief Inspector Simon Whitman, of the London Metropolitan Police, said today, 'We are treating this as a murder investigation. Due to the enormous profile of one of the victims we will not be releasing any further details at this time.'

The football world has been rocked by this devastating twist as the search for the 24-year-old Authenton FC star has come to an end. Kieran Ledley, widely regarded as the best football player of his generation, had been missing for two days. He sensationally went AWOL hours before his club's FA Cup Final clash against Tarrington United, which they went on to lose 3–0. Fans turned against their star player, accusing him of 'bottling it' and thinking that he was bigger than the football club. There were wild reports about his whereabouts, including rumours that he had escaped to Las Vegas to marry his long-term girlfriend Clarissa Harvey, of the pop group Girl-Fiends. There were even suggestions that he had been kidnapped in an act of revenge against his stepbrother, 27-year-old former gang member Callum Ledley, who was released from prison last year.

Hundreds of tributes have been left outside the cordoned-off hotel, which has been closed during the investigation.

There have also been several hundred flowers and messages left in honour of the star outside Authenton's training ground. The club's owners, the Karim brothers, are due to arrive at Authenton FC's stadium from the Middle East by private jet later today.

One distraught fan at the training ground shrine said, 'I cannot believe this. It feels like a dream. It's like a movie.'

Another, 18-year-old Kyle Davis, said, 'He was my hero. Even when he went missing, I knew something was up. But there are always rumours about him, so it's hard to know what to believe.'

Club Chairman Donald Kleens, 48, released a statement earlier that read: 'We are deeply saddened by the sudden loss of such a gifted athlete. It is extremely hard to put into words our utter devastation at the nature of Kieran Ledley's death. Our prayers go out to his family, fiancée and friends at this incredibly difficult time.'

While his talent was never disputed, Kieran Ledley had become somewhat of a divisive figure over the past few years. To many he was a magician on the pitch with an unmatched first touch, was frighteningly fast, and had the ability to win a game on his own.

To some he was an unfaithful playboy, with a long-suffering pop star girlfriend. A young man who lived the fast life, with a love of women and sports cars. With reported earnings of over £200,000 a week, he was the highest-paid football player in the world.

The striker was born Kieran Jermane Ledley on 8th September 1987, in Camden North London.

Anna and Nigel Ledley – Nigel who tragically died last year when he was on the way to watch Kieran play in Authenton's match against Daggerton Rovers – adopted Kieran.

He grew up with his stepbrother, Callum.

Kieran, whose biological parents are of British and Jamaican origin, had a somewhat difficult time at school. While growing up he was racially abused and suffered taunts because a white family had taken him in.

His agent, Nathan Rougel, who spotted him playing football with his brother in a park, guided Kieran's career. In a 2004 interview, after Kieran had won his first cap for England, Nathan said, 'This is the proudest day of my life. Kieran is like a son to me.'

The player went on to be capped 67 times for his country, scoring 24 goals. He played at the 2004 European Championships and scored 3 goals. Ledley featured at the 2006 and 2010 World Cups, and was due to lead the line for England at this summer's European tournament.

During his career he won the English Player of the Year Award three times, in 2006, 2009 and 2010, and had recently been crowned World Player of the Year.

Aged 10, Ledley joined the youth team of Albans Town, for whom he made his debut in 2003, becoming the youngest player to appear in the Premier League. He spent an incredible eight seasons at the club before joining Authenton FC for a staggering £70 million in the summer transfer window of 2011. His 38 goals this season led the team to their first championship since 2006.

Kieran's mother, Anna, is thought to be too distressed to speak. She is said to be currently being comforted by relatives at the family home. The star's agent, Nathan Rougel, could not be reached for comment, but Clarissa's spokeswoman, Louise D'Orazio, has issued a statement saying, 'We understand the huge interest in this case. But we ask that you respect the family's privacy during this difficult period. With the death of Kieran's father, Nigel, last year, it has been a hellacious chapter for the Ledley's. Kieran's family and Clarissa ask for time to grieve.'

VIVIAN

There was a knock at the door. Vivian folded the newspaper and tucked it into her desk draw.

She looked at her reflection in the mirror and reminded herself that she needed to regain her composure. 'Fifth wall, Vivian,' she muttered to herself. 'Just a second,' she called as she adjusted her short hair. She walked over to her desk, took a deep breath, and said, 'Come in.'

In walked her newest patient, Daniel Martins.

Thank you very much for reading this book. I hope you enjoyed it (and got to this page organically by reading the whole thing - I said this at the end of my first book and I'm saying it again because it's true!). Please be so kind as to follow the simple steps and leave a review on Amazon or Goodreads. Whilst all writers can't deny the influence of critics, the voice of the people is a lot more important to me! Thanks again, and I truly value your support :) Michael

ABOUT THE AUTHOR

Michael Obiora was born in North-West London to Nigerian parents. At ten years old he landed a lead part in the hit children's school drama Grange Hill. He went on to appear in such programmes as Sea of Souls, Judge John Deed, Dr Who, Afterlife, The BAFTA award winning Misfits, and My Family. His stage work includes the lead roles in the award-winning plays Fallout at the Royal Court Theatre and Elmina's Kitchen at the Garrick Theatre in London's West End. It is for his roles as flamboyant receptionist 'Ben Trueman' in BBC1's smash hit Hotel Babylon, and 'Lloyd Asike' in long-running BAFTA award winning medical drama Casualty that Michael is best known. Upcoming television projects include Sky Atlantic's 2015 twelve-part crime thriller Fortitude.

Michael is a keen Arsenal fan, enjoys travelling, food, and an eclectic mix of music - especially Gangsta Rap. He lives in London with his wife.

You can keep up with his writing at www.michaelobiora.com

Also by Michael Obiora

Black Shoes: Reality Check

Meet successful London property developer **Daniel Martins**. He has everything a man could want: his own booming business, the luxury pad, the expensive sports car... all at the tender age of twenty-five. But should he appreciate this more because he is black...?

Praise for Black Shoes

"BLACK SHOES offers a welcome relief from the "ghetto lit" being rung through cash registers across the UK... Ghetto lit will do well to take a leaf out of that book and walk a step or two in Obiora's Black Shoes." Aaron Akinyemi, *The Guardian*

"...it's surprising that Black Shoes is Obiora's first novel as he probes and wrestles with Daniel's character like someone who has been writing for years... reveals a complicated, layered and three dimensional character in Daniel. A morality tale, with more than a ring of truth to it for modern Britain – this is a great start for the actor/author." **Lime Magazine**

"Obiora is a promising writer. This is more than entertainment, what transpires is a thought-provoking debut in the so called "post racial", post-Obama election era." **The New Black Magazine**

"The narrative of Black Shoes powers along in short, rapid shifts that build up to a powerful climax" **Property Week**